shoes

tails from the post

R. A. Comunale, M.D.

Safehaven Books
McLean, Virginia

shoes: tails from the post

© 2013 R.A. Comunale, M.D.

Published by Safehaven Books

Library of Congress Control Number 2013941683

ISBN 978-0-9885919-5-0

Printed in the United States of America

Cover concept by R.A. Comunale

Cover by David Knowles

Book design by Michael Hentges

Contents

PART II: **shoes**

To the Cadet Corps of VMI

Foreword

Ducks and dykes.

Y'all sure use some strange terms.

I freely admit that I am not an alumnus of Virginia Military Institute, nor have I ever attended.

That was my loss.

My Rubenesque body would not have survived the tough discipline and workouts.

My introduction to VMI—my personal Virgil—is an alumnus who chooses to be known only as Leonidas. Like the Spartan king of old, he soon conquered my reservations about visiting a campus dedicated to both education and military preparedness.

Leonidas approached me one day with a suggestion for a novel centered on VMI. On his own time he conveyed me to the Post, showed me the landmarks, and recounted his own experiences as a young Rat. He showed me the farm, where the great battle of New Market took place, and related what I only knew briefly: the bravery and courage of an entire Corps of Cadets.

He also related some of the historical background of Lexington and Buena Vista, Virginia.

He then wisely told me, "It's all yours. Run with it."

I hope you enjoy it.

shoes

PART I
chestnuts

Prologue

GENESIS 22:1-24

"Where are we going, Papa?"

"Climb up on my shoulders, boy."

"But where are we going?"

"To the mountaintop."

"Why?"

"To see God."

Hegira

I was a moth pinned to the hospital bed by IV tubes.

The thread of my life echoed in the repetitive low pitched bugle note of the heart monitor.

Is that all there is?

Damn, Peggy Lee had it right.

Was it only just a few weeks ago…?

"Bye, Dad, see you on Fall Break."

My daughter stood on her toes to kiss me on the cheek. My five-foot, ten-inch frame was no challenge to my little girl.

Little girl? She's a senior in college now.

Does time really pass that quickly?

"Dad, what's that spot on your neck?"

"Huh, what spot, Krissie?"

My beautiful, twenty-one-year-old daughter led me like a child by the hand to the hallway mirror in my apartment near Dulles Airport.

I stared at the one-inch, red and black spot, its irregular borders reaching out like some distorted crab across my skin.

She rubbed her fingers over it then suddenly pulled her hand away.

"Dad, didn't you notice these bumps?"

I moved my hand over my neck and felt the cobblestones of death.

"When was the last time you saw a doctor?"

"I had my flight physical six months ago on a layover in Chicago"

"So your regular medical examiner didn't see you."

"No."

She knew her old man was a commercial pilot. She also knew that I had to be checked out medically every six months in order to fly the big birds.

"Kristin, it wasn't there six months ago. I'm sure of it."

"Come on, Dad, let's go see Doctor Galen."

"I don't have an appointment."

"Has he ever turned you away?"

"No."

The heavy-set old man had been my AME, aviation medical examiner, for as long as I had lived in Northern Virginia. Normally he would greet me with bad jokes and insults. It was what endeared him to pilots too numerous to count.

Not this time.

"It's melanoma, Gus."

"Cancer?"

"Yes."

"Dr. Galen, how bad does Dad have it?"

The old doctor's forehead was creased.

"It's already spread to his liver and brain, Miss Belmont."

"How long do I have, doc?"

Where's Kristin? Come on, girl. Don't let your old man fade out alone in this hospital.

You're not alone, Gus.

"Wha…? Who said that?"

My tongue stuck dry inside my mouth.

"I … I can't see you."

Not yet.

"Am I dying?"

Yes.

"Must be the drugs they're pumpin' into me. You're not real, Voice. But, just for the hell of it, I'll play along. It's better than waiting to die. Oh, what the hell, what's the use. Who'm I kidding?

"You know, Voice, when I die, nothing will change. My life's a cipher. I've never done anything worth remembering."

You've got a beautiful daughter, Gus. Wasn't that worth it?

"Dear God, yes, but… Hey, are you God?"

No, sir.

"Was that a kid? Hey, Voice, is he yours?"

Come on, Gus, you know him, too.

"Okay, so I don't remember. What's your name, kid?"

Don't you know, sir?

Augustus Belmont—"Gus," they called me. I closed my eyes. I could not escape my past.

In the Beginning Was

"Papa, why did we come to the mountain?"

"Hush, my son, I must pray to God."

"But mama says you are having bad dreams."

"O God of Abraham, I believe. Forgive me my unbelief."

"Why are you crying, Papa?"

"He looks like a penguin!"

My daughter had never been to my old alma mater, Virginia Military Institute. Her mother, my ex, had never wanted her daughter exposed to "such stuff."

But here we were, back at The Post.

It was Kristin's idea.

"I want to spend my off time with you."

She didn't need to say "in your last days, Dad."

"I thought you and your mother were going to Europe on fall break."

It was Kristin's senior year at William and Mary. I couldn't have asked for a better daughter. Athletic, bright, five feet six, one-hundred-sixteen pounds of head-turning, eye-ogling classic Grecian face, topped by glistening blonde hair and blue-gray eyes. She could have her pick of the college boys in heat.

But this was her idea.

"Dad, why don't we take a road trip together? We can visit all your old hangouts; it'll be a trip down memory lane."

"What are you going to tell your mom?"

"That I promised Renee I'd go with her to Narragansett."

Renee was her roommate and BFF (best friend forever).

My ex and I were married fourteen years. I had met Sandy out west my second year in the Air Force. As any fly guy will tell you, women find us irresistible.

Yeah, right.

I was twenty four, flying C130s, the troop and cargo transport ships of the skies. Every time I climbed in one of those birds, my mind took off on wings of memory, of a time when I knew and loved that one special woman in my life.

No, it wasn't Sandy.

Oh, I loved my wife in many ways. We were young. She was a teacher at the base school and we were both twenty-four and unattached. I considered myself lucky to be picked by the auburn-haired, green-eyed slender girl who sought my help fixing a flat tire on her car just off base.

It wasn't a whirlwind romance. We actually tested ourselves for a whole six months before finding a J.P. (justice of the peace) and sealing the deal. Twelve months later, it was me, Sandy and baby Kristin.

We moved around a bit over the next ten years, our housing improving as my military status went to bird-colonel level. But Sandy had dreams of moving east and, I guess, so did I. My roots were in Ohio and my post high school education in Virginia.

Tornadoes, dust storms and droughts were not my cup of tea. And, despite my love of flying, neither were the frequent away times when I had temporary posting in innumerable mid-eastern and Asian bases, ferrying troops into whatever local conflict we were engaged in.

shoes

It was the opening position at a commercial airline that had clinched the deal.

Year twelve found us in Northern Virginia with me a civilian for the first time since I'd started college. Sandy readily found work as an E.S.L. (English as a second language) teacher. Her linguistic skills in Spanish, honed by the numerous immigrant waves along the U.S. southwestern border areas, were a big plus in the hiring process.

Our little girl, our Kristin, would have been at home anywhere, even on the moon. She never ceased to amaze Sandy and me with her adaptability and acceptance of change.

I watched her blossom into a young woman in the Virginia climate.

Things seemed to be ideal until…

"I want a divorce, Gus."

It was Kristin's fourteenth birthday. She had blown out the candles on her cake—chocolate mousse, if I remember correctly—and she and her friends had gone outside to yack and text as only teenage girls can do.

I was helping Sandy clear the debris produced by eight fourteen-year-olds and two adults from the dining room in our Reston, Virginia, home.

I looked up and saw my wife standing there, giving me one of her intense looks.

All husbands know that look. You can never tell if your spouse is going to start an argument, present a problem with the kids, or just … because.

"You want a horse? Why?"

I thought it was a joke.

She came closer.

"Gus, I want a divorce."

I never quite understood why she wanted to break up. All she did was to repeat over and over that she needed to find herself.

What could I say? "Is it something I said or did? I thought everything was going great, Sandy."

She shook her head and ran to our bedroom, locking the door behind her.

I turned and saw Kristin standing in the open patio doorway, crying.

She ran to me, and I held her.

It was amicable. We shared joint custody of our only child, but it was never the same for me.

I blamed myself. My job kept me away a lot. I guess I still blame myself.

And, deep down, I still remembered my first love—Lauren.

"Dad, did you hear what I said?"

"Huh? Oh, yeah, Krissie…"

My mind had done some time traveling while my daughter was speaking to me.

"You sure you want to spend your vacation with an old man?"

A nod of the head and a kiss on my cheek—it was settled.

It wasn't a long journey. From Northern Virginia, Interstate 66 winds gently west to Interstate 81's southwesterly heading. Three hours of rolling farms and mountain ranges later we were on the outskirts of the Blue Ridge Mountains.

"Your old man used to spend a lot of off-time in those hills, girl."

"Why?"

How could I tell her? How do I describe what college life was like at a military institute with the reputation and renown of VMI? You can't know unless you've lived it.

We threaded our way up and down mountain roads and finally turned off Route 60 and climbed the hill to the entryway to my past.

Tawny yellow buildings, stark and spare, lined the way and I felt the same shiver that a not-quite eighteen-year-old Gus Belmont felt when the boy that was my past first saw the Post on the outskirts of Lexington, Virginia.

We pulled up in front of the Stonewall Jackson Arch, one of the four gateway arches to the five-story barracks that housed the men and women of the Corps. I felt a bit weak as I opened the car door but that familiar mountaintop breeze that had once meant both pleasure and pain rejuvenated me.

"Did you dress like that?"

Kristin caught her first glimpse of what I wore for four years of my life: white ducks—trousers—and gray tunic.

"Yep, and, not to brag, daughter, but I looked damned good in them, too."

She laughed as she looked at my still-lean frame then gasped as an obviously new cadet came running past, arms braced at his sides, back stiff in what we then affectionately called the straining position—the one she had said looked like a penguin.

"Dad, what's wrong with him?"

"He's a Rat, Kristin. It's his first year, and he and his classmates are still not fully accepted yet. In another couple of months, he will be. But for now, he's still in what we called the Rat Line and has to endure some damned hard discipline to prove he's worthy of being a VMI cadet and member of the Corps."

"You had to do this?"

"Yes."

God yes, girl. And stuff I can't even tell you about yet.

I turned and exercised my right as an alumnus.

"Out of the Rat Line, cadet."

Instantly the kid's shoulders relaxed even as he continued to run toward his destination.

We walked through the archway after I notified the guard on duty at the office.

"That's where I lived."

She stared at the inner courtyard and the five-storied barracks with their balconied stoops and cast iron outside stairways leading to each floor.

The wind rose and banshee howled through the archways.

Is that a snare drum roll I hear?

The stoops suddenly filled with cadets wrapped in blankets.

Where did the sunlight go?

I see them marching in, single file, fifteen men and women.

Oh, my God, I see myself … and Lauren.

And then I hear the words that struck terror through all of us, even those who participated in the decision.

Court, ten-hut!

Court, fall in.

Tonight your Honor Court has met. After a trial hearing, it has found Cadet Ashburn, Donald R., guilty of cheating. He has left the institution, never to return, and his name will not be mentioned within the four walls of barracks again.

"Dad, what's wrong?"

My knees buckled and suddenly two cadets are holding me up.

It's daylight once more.

"I'm … I'm okay now."

My voice was shaky. Even I could hear the tremor.

"Sir, do you need medical attention?"

"Uh … no, thank you, cadet. Just an old man reliving the past. I'll be all right. Come on, Kristin, let's go back outside."

My first steps were unsteady but then I found my cadence.

"Wanna see the old man march?"

"Quit joking, Dad. Let's go back to the car."

"Wait. There are a few more things I want to show you."

We walked across the narrow turnaround street in front of the castle-like barracks and approached the statue of Thomas "Stonewall" Jackson. There he stood on his stone pylon, facing the parade grounds, defended by four ancient artillery pieces.

"Let me introduce you to Matthew, Mark, Luke, and John."

"What?"

"The artillery pieces."

"The cannons?"

I nodded then saluted old Stonewall.

"Come on, we'll drive through the rest of the Post. But first, I've got a surprise for you."

I opened the hatchback trunk of our SUV and smiled as my daughter saw what lay inside.

"Camping gear!"

My little girl loved camping. Her mother never did. She said the military housing she grew up in was camping enough for her; but the last time we vacationed together as a family was a camping trip—something Kristin pleaded to do for her twelfth birthday.

My wife's face could have turned cucumbers into pickles the day we took the old family car down the road for a weekend campout in the cabins near Potomac Falls.

Truth be told, it wasn't a camp out with tents and bags for Sandy and me. She would never have agreed to that. But Kristin, now a full-fledged girl scout, brought her own tent and stuff while my wife and I roughed it inside an air-conditioned cabin with cable TV.

I guess my little girl inherited that love of outdoors from my side of the genetic crap shoot.

"Where are we going camping, Dad?"

"Uh-uh, not yet. I haven't shown you the rest of the Post."

"Why do you keep calling it that? Isn't it a campus?"

"Tradition."

We drove past the classroom buildings and Crozet Hall, where I got indigestion those critical first four months learning to eat what we called square meals, a unique torture imposed on Rats.

"Ever eat a square meal, Krissie?"

She gagged as I told her how we had to brace upright while sitting down and move our arms in right angle motions to bring food to our mouths.

"How can anyone live like that?'

We did. It taught us discipline, self-control, and something most civilians can't appreciate: *esprit de corps*.

Our car passed an all-too-familiar classroom building with blacked out windows on an upper level room. Kristin didn't notice it, and I said nothing as we drove on.

The snare drum beat a farewell tattoo that only I could hear.

Chestnuts

October, 1891

"Are you still having the bad dream, Edwin?"

"Yes, Lillian That little coffin in that black wagon … I can't stop it. The blackness, the overwhelming blackness and cold!"

November 9, 1891

"Ottie, would you like to go with the other boys and gather some wood for the stove?"

"Oh, yes, Miss Gilbert!"

The potbellied stove in the one-room school was turning cold as the wood fire within burned to a cinder.

"Now, be careful. Put your shoes and coat on. It's cold outside. And here are three chestnuts to eat."

"Thank you, Miss Gilbert."

"Listen to the older boys, Ottie."

"Hey, guys, a penny fer the one with the biggest stick!"

"Can I play, too?"

"Naw, yer too little. G'wan over there."

"Why can't I play, Marty?"

"Git, runt!"

"I'll show you! Just wait."

He knew where there was a really big stick. He had seen it while riding on his papa's shoulders the day they visited the mountaintop.

"Papa, what's that over there?"

"Never mind, boy, we've got more important things to do than worry about an old chestnut branch. Now, hold on, tight, son."

It couldn't be too far. It had to be over that way. Or was it over there?

"Where's Ottie, Martin?"

"Uh, I dunno, Miss Gilbert. He didn' wanna stay with us."

"Ottie … Ottie … come on back to school!"

She rang the hand-held brass and wood handled bell ubiquitous among schoolmarms.

"Ottie, where are you?"

The Present

"Dad, what are all those dead trees on the mountains?"

My daughter had never seen American chestnut trees. Most people haven't. At one time there were great forests across our country. The chestnut provided edible nuts and beautifully grained wood.

Then, like me, a blight hit in the early twentieth century and the trees died by the millions.

Occasionally a sucker would grow from a dead tree's roots, but after seeming to survive for a number of years, it, too, died.

"These were once magnificent American chestnut trees, Krissie. They died a long time ago."

Bluff Mountain

"Dad, slow down!"

Kristin and I had just belched our way through some fast food in Lexington and I was anxious to move on. So much to do and so little time: I had to double-time march through what life I had left.

"Wait, Dad. Let me get a souvenir. Look at that little antique shop over there!"

I pulled the car to the curb. Kristin got out, almost running to the old store window. She peered at the jewelry displayed on faded black velvet—mostly junk.

"Dad, look at the oval gold locket in the little window case."

"Hmpff, probably the only decent thing in the shop," I snorted.

I have to admit, it was pretty. About two inches by one inch, with flower-covered tree branches engraving along both sides, it reminded me of my mother's keepsake locket that held my Dad's and my pictures in it.

I didn't recognize the flowers.

"I'm going to buy it, okay?"

Translation: buy it for me.

That surprised me. My Kristin was not the type of girl who went gaga over jewelry. A new hockey stick or a pair of riding boots—in a heartbeat. But bling-bling? Nah.

"What's so special about it, Krissie?"

"I don't know, Dad. It just seems to want me."

I'd heard that before, too. Cats, dogs, even birds and frogs seemed to "want" my daughter. When she was little, she used to say that her "friend," the one only she could see, wanted her to have them.

What the hell, why not? I'd already spent a wad on the camping gear. Besides, what good was money going to do me?

I had gone to the lawyer. Everything was set up. What was left when I was … well … gone? Kristin would be taken care of. My ex could live off the guy she was hanging around with at the moment.

The door chimed as we entered the hole-in-the-wall shop that should probably have called itself junk instead of antique.

"May I help you folks?"

The woman sitting on the chair was elderly but could still see well enough to wonder if I was some old goat hitting on a young chippy. I could see her hazel eyes constrict as she looked, first at Kristin and then at me.

Kristin was bubbling over. "May I see the locket in the window, the little oval one engraved with flowers?"

The old woman hesitated then smiled, as she rose slowly from a bentwood rocker and took a key from her gray blouse pocket. She went to the window case, unlocked it, picked up the locket and set it on a black rubber mat.

"It's beautiful. Ma'am, what type of flowers are these?"

"Chestnut catkins."

"Oh, Dad, I really want it."

I did my best not to smirk, as the old woman's face relaxed.

"Your daughter?"

"Yes, ma'am. Uh … how much for the locket?"

"It's gold, you know. Should be three-fifty, but the catch seems to be broken. Can't open it, so … one-seventy-five?"

I gulped silently then took out my wallet. You get used to that with kids, especially daughters. I gave her my credit card. Ten seconds later I was signing a charge slip.

The shopkeeper smiled and looked at Kristin "You at W and L?"

She meant Washington and Lee, the other school at the top of the hill where VMI and its predecessor arsenal had stood for almost two hundred years.

"Oh, no, ma'am, I'm at William and Mary. My dad and I are just revisiting his old alma mater."

Her eyes narrowed again. "VMI?"

"Yes, ma'am."

I thought she was going to spit on me.

"Had a nephew there. Got expelled his last year under their so-called Honor Code, supposedly fer cheatin'. He always said he didn't do it."

"I'm sorry to hear that, ma'am, but the Honor Code is pretty specific. A cadet will not lie, cheat, steal, or tolerate those who do so."

"Donnie Ashburn were his name. Boy killed hisself the next day. My sister went to her grave 'cause of it."

A snare drum resounded in my head.

"Kristin, I think we'd better leave."

"Uh … okay, Dad. Thanks for the locket."

I almost ran out the door, my daughter trying to keep up with me.

"What's wrong? Is it something I said?"

"No … no, not at all. I guess that woman doesn't have much use for VMI and I could feel it."

"Dad, come on, it's more than that. What's going on?"

I couldn't tell her. Not yet–but when? How does one tell his daughter, "Kristin, I was on the jury that convicted that old woman's nephew."

Did I just blurt that out? I looked at my daughter and saw the light of understanding in her eyes

"Krissie, it's true."

I got back in the SUV I had rented. My old Toyota wouldn't have been able to go where I was headed next. Kristin sat next to me in the front seat, not replying to my stilted banter. She kept rubbing the little locket as if it was Aladdin's lamp.

"Dad, about that old woman, was her nephew really guilty?"

"Krissie, you have to know what an Honor Court is and how it's run. All of us serve and try our best not to convict, but sometimes the evidence leaves us no choice."

She nodded then fell silent again.

I kept the windows closed as we rolled through the countryside. It was still warm down in the valley, but I felt a chill course through me as I thought of that day twenty five years ago, when I sat on a jury with…

"Look at that! There are initials engraved on the back: L.C.P. Wonder who she was."

The case gleamed in the sunlight piercing the coated windows of the car. She kept rubbing it, and suddenly it split like two halves of a walnut hinged together. Inside was a tiny lock of chestnut brown hair, the fine hair that only a child possesses.

"What's that?"

Kristin was startled.

I pulled the SUV to the side and took the locket from her.

I knew, but wondered if I should tell her.

"Kristin, it's a memento mori locket. Back in the days when people died young and suddenly, the family would take a lock of the dead person's hair and keep it as a reminder of that person. Children died early from all sorts of infections we can deal with today. It was not uncommon for a mother to keep a lock of her dead child's hair."

She closed the locket then shut her eyes, the golden shell held tightly in her hand.

We drove in silence along Route 60 until I found the ramp to the Blue Ridge Parkway. I could feel my ears popping a bit as we drove up along the mountain road. Then I pulled over.

"Why are we stopping?"

"Take a look, Kristin. Isn't that an amazing view?"

I had stopped at a familiar spot. It was a scenic overlook of the valley. The sign read: BLUFF MOUNTAIN ALTITUDE 3300 FEET.

"Look. Over there's Lexington. And that way is Buena Vista. Can you make out the school from here?"

Gus, look, did you ever see anything so beautiful?

No, Lauren.

How many times had we held hands, staring down from that very spot?

The remnants of dead tree trunks lay scattered on the slope.

"Okay, back in the car, Krissie. It's not far now."

"Where are we headed?"

"Mother Nature's Motel."

There it was, unchanged in twenty-five years. I pulled off the paved highway onto a graveled dirt road fit only for four-wheel drive and forced the SUV even higher. Finally we came to a cast iron post in the middle of the old fire road.

"That's a strange place to put a pole."

She was miffed at the sudden obstruction in our upward flight. My daughter was never one to let obstacles stand in her way. Even as a baby, she could climb out of childproof cribs and weasel her way past gates meant to keep her safe from stairs.

"I guess the park rangers don't want people trying to drive to the summit in their Cadillacs. Can you imagine trying to tow one of those out of here?

Okay, it's shank's mare from here, daughter. We're about two-thirds up Bluff Mountain. Come on, let's grab our gear. Wait'll you see the camp site."

It was mid-fall. Down in the valley, grass lawns dotted with impatiens and pansies gloried in the midday sun. It was balmy despite the cross-breezes off the surrounding peaks. But up here, almost at the summit, the chill of fall and a winter yet to come were evident. Mountain flora were still peeking up from the rocky soil, but the mountain laurel and stunted wild rhododendrons were turning brown-flecked from the nighttime cold. The Jackson oaks and chestnut suckers that sprouted from the blight-plagued stumps of once glorious American chestnut trees were displaying their reds, ochres and browns, while the valley trees still kept their chlorophyll greens.

It always amazed me how trees dead before the Great War still tried a hopeless resurrection.

I was surprised how heavy my pack felt as I shifted it onto my back. Kristin easily flipped hers up and over and I snugged the straps for her. There was a time when I could carry both packs: mine and Lauren's.

We followed the jeep-rutted fire trail up about three hundred yards, until we hit the fork. Straight ahead, maybe another five hundred yards, was the summit. To our left was an open field.

"It may be a bit wet, so follow in my footsteps."

We trudged to the left across fall-dying haygrass and arrived at a copse of scrub trees. To the right was an outhouse.

"There it is: the Punch Bowl!"

The small pond lay shimmering in the reflected sunlight. No birds now, but it served as a way station for migratory birds and a watering trough for the indigenous white-tail deer. Both would avoid the times when humans invaded their haunts.

It was also a great place for college-age kids to look at the moon and … well, you know. I still remembered the last time I was here, Lauren riding behind me on a borrowed motorbike as we snuck off-post that late Saturday for an overnight campout.

Behind the copse was a three-sided hiker's shelter.

"Mother Nature's Motel—free room, no board."

Kristin hugged me. "I love it already!"

Then she turned. "Do kids play up here?"

"Don't think so. Why?"

"I thought I saw a little boy running over that way. Must be the tree shadows."

I stared at her as she turned and headed for the shelter. Was it happening again?

Sometimes both my ex and I were unnerved by our little girl, as she sat and talked for hours to no one in particular. The shrinks said it was normal for kids to have an invisible playmate at some point in their young lives. So we laughed and smiled and pretended to talk to her "friends."

Then, one day, it stopped. We asked our little girl what had happened to them, and she just smiled and said they had gone somewhere else.

I followed her. I couldn't keep her pace so I called out, "hey, slow down!"

Kristin turned and smiled as I huffed and puffed up to her.

"Let's put our gear in the shelter. Then I want to show you something."

The unspoken law of hikers: No one steals another person's gear. It's the Honor Code of the mountain.

Suddenly I felt totally drained.

"Kris, let's go rest in the shelter a bit then maybe we'll head up to the summit. It's quite a view."

She gave me the look. It wasn't her mother's look; Kristin's showed concern, worry, not the cynicism in my ex's eyes.

"Sure you don't want to lie down in the SUV, Dad?"

"Daughter, do you know what I slept on for four years at VMI?"

She giggled. "Girls?"

I know, I know, she's all grown up. But fathers still look at their daughters and see the five-year-old who climbed up on their shoulders and caused heart attacks by hanging upside down from tree limbs.

I blushed and harrumphed.

"I'll have you know we slept on our hay, girl; hard, uncomfortable mats right on the floor. We didn't have namby-pamby foam mattresses like the kids at W and L, or William and Mary, for that matter."

"Yes, sir, Cap'n sir."

She did a half-assed salute and we both laughed until I started to choke.

By three o'clock the air was slightly warmer as the direct sun's rays through the half-bare trees had heated things up. I had rebounded from my enervation and wanted to show Kristin the summit. I also wanted to surprise her.

"Feel up to being a mountain goat, girl?"

"Only if the older goat goes first!"

She truly was my daughter.

Once more, we left the shelter and our gear and headed back to the fork in the road. I had to force myself but I walked up the ever-increasing grade of the fire road. I was covered in sweat as we hit the top.

Back after World War I, the government built a fire tower for the rangers to observe the surrounding forests. Long gone now, only the concrete pylons remained. But there was something else up there that I hadn't told Kristin about.

"What's that over there?"

We approached the little concrete marker with its bronze plaque inscription.

Kristin stared at it then began to read out loud:

"This is the exact spot on which Ottie Cline Powell's body was found April 5, 1891 after straying away from Tower Hill School House Nov. 9. A distance of 7 miles. Age 4 years, 11 months."

She dropped to her knees and moved her hands over the inscription. She was crying.

"What happened to him, Dad?"

I helped her up. We walked over to one of the decaying concrete fire tower pylons and sat down.

"The dates on the marker are wrong but there really was a little boy named Ottie. He wasn't quite five years old that November 9th, 1891."

Papa, papa, can I stay home and help you with the corn shucking?

"Little Ottie was the sixth of what would ultimately be eight children from Edwin and Lillian Cline Powell. His father was a farmer and a minister of the Dunkard religion.

"From what was recorded later, Edwin admitted that he had forcibly told the boy to go to school, something for which, the neighbors said, his wife never forgave him. He never forgave himself, either.

"Ottie was probably the youngest boy in the little one-room Tower Hill School House run by Nannie Gilbert.

"That day Nannie sent the boys out at recess to gather kindling wood for the wood-burning stove. Ottie went with them. But when the boys returned, he was not among them. When the teacher finally realized that one of her charges was missing she sent the boys out again to look for him and to summon help.

"They found the twelve-foot-long chestnut tree branch that Ottie had tried to drag back to the school but, despite hundreds of searchers, never found him.

"That night it rained and turned to ice up on the mountain.

"Now, here's the strange thing: The following April, at this very spot on top of Bluff Mountain, four young hunters found little Ottie's body. Except for the feet being eaten, probably by wild animals, the boy did not seem to be harmed.

"A local doctor did what was considered an autopsy and found three undigested chestnuts in the boy's stomach. He declared that little Ottie had died of exposure that first day he went missing.

"What's wrong with that picture, Kristin?"

"How did he get up here?"

"That's right! The town folk felt that the boy, in panic and terror, ran and ran until he reached the top of the mountain, then lay down, exhausted, and fell asleep. He never woke up.

"The thing that has bothered me since I first read about his case is the distance. It's seven miles up from that school house down in the valley. Even grown men have trouble navigating the old Indian and animal trails, much less running wildly through brambles and other obstructions. In fact, the hunters who did find him had initially bypassed the area a week before because of difficulty traversing the Old Bear Trail which leads through here."

Kristin was wide-eyed.

"Do you think he was killed?"

I shook my head. "I don't know. Everyone felt that the doctor's findings of undigested chestnuts in the boy's stomach meant that he had died only about three hours after getting lost. Could a panicked not-quite-five-year-old child walk seven miles up a mountain in that time?

"If he was killed, was he carried up there? And, if so, why?"

"Dad, that poor little boy! There's got to be an answer!"

"Krissie, remember when I read you the story about Peter Pan and the Lost Boys?"

She nodded.

"Well, I like to think that little Ottie is with Peter and those other boys. But my rational mind says otherwise."

Kristin leaned her head on my shoulder, just as she did as a little girl, and stared at that tiny marker.

Lauren

Lauren, why did you leave me?

We were candy-cane fragments melting in the August heat.

Dressed in our Hell Week red gym shorts and white tee shirts, we stood in line, some smiling, some silently crying as parents and friends waved at us.

It was our first day at VMI.

"Dad, wake up. What's wrong?"

I sat straight up. Not an easy thing to do in a sleeping bag.

The evening air was chilly despite the little fire my daughter had started in the stone circle fire pit. I hadn't realized how tired I was until we climbed back down from the summit and trudged over to the shelter. I must have just unfolded my bag and climbed in. The next thing I remember, Kristin was shaking me.

"Wha … what happened?"

"You were tossing and turning and calling out for someone named Lauren."

She looked me straight in the eye.

"Who is she? Is that why you and mom split up?"

I shook my head. I felt nauseated in doing so. The flickering tongues of flame doubled then resolved into one image.

"No, no, it was long before I met your mother. Truth be told, Lauren would have been your mother if she hadn't … she hadn't…"

I couldn't seem to focus. My head pounded and the nausea rose within me. I managed to lean over and upchucked the entire contents of that earlier fast-food meal. I felt embarrassed. Parents aren't supposed to get sick or show weakness.

"Come on, Dad, Let's go home. I'll drive."

"No, no. I'm okay."

Maybe it was getting rid of the food, but I did feel better. Food poisoning? Or was my pigmented crab, my growing partner within, messing with my brain?

"Don't you want to hear about Lauren?"

She hesitated then sat down, Indian style, as I lay back and stared up at the shelter roof.

"It was almost thirty years ago. I had just arrived in Lexington, Virginia. My parents and I drove up the hill to my future home, Virginia Military Institute—VMI."

Welcome, new cadets.

"We stood there in civvies for the last time. Your grandparents, Grandpa Julius and Grandma Libby, watched as I waited in Cameron Hall to sign the matriculation book. It was my commitment to what lay ahead. Then I was told to change into the special outfit that would be both insignia and badge of shame: red shorts and white tee shirt. "I was a farm boy, a damned good one, too. Our Ohio spread had been in the family for almost one hundred years. My older brothers worked it with my dad and, until I reached my teens, I thought I would, too.

"Not that you would know it, daughter, but I was pretty damned smart in school. Top grades in math and science and one helluva competitive wrestler. My coach hinted that I should try for some military scholarships and told me about some internet sites.

"From the moment I logged in, I fell in love with the Virginia Military Institute.

"It wasn't easy, but I had the grades, and I was physically fit—a rare combination in those days!

"I saw my father's sunburned face and my mother dabbing at her eyes as we were told to line up and fall into a truly half-assed semblance of military formation.

"I saw someone else as well.

"She was just a bit taller than I was. High cheek bones, long black hair, still uncut—yes, we got shaved to the nub later—and olive complexion highlighted by piercing dark eyes. She … she … filled her shorts and shirt in a special way.

"Okay, she turned me on! Stop laughing, Krissie.

"And thank God, I entered VMI after women were allowed to matriculate."

"Allowed?"

I saw my daughter's eyebrows rise. Better explain real quick, or I would get an earful.

"Well, until the latter part of the twentieth century, the major military academies allowed only men to enter. It took several landmark cases, among them one against VMI, before women were allowed to enter as cadets. Since then, VMI has been in the forefront of training top-notch women cadets and those graduates have served our country well.

"Now, where was I?"

"It was your first day. You were in socks and jocks, marching, and saw this girl."

"Don't be a wiseass, kiddo, you know it was red gym shorts and tee shirt.

"Anyway, I stumbled as the upper classman assigned as our drill instructor, Torquemada, our Cadre, started yelling commands as we marched to barracks.

"I didn't care. My mind was on only one thing. That girl was Pocahontas and Minnehaha rolled into one."

God a'mighty, did you smell our DI's breath?

"We were five in our room. Our hay, the mattresses we would sleep on, were still rolled up. And we were drenched in sweat."

Don't think none a' us smell that good, guys.

"Our outfits were soaked. Non-stop running, push-ups, sit-ups, obstacle courses and log lifting do that to you. No wonder they told us to eat and drink lots of fluids that last normal meal.

"We ran to the showers, navels to asses, and rinsed off as quickly as we could. The word had come down: Be prepared for some fun at 11 p.m.

"Ah, yes, our Cadre would show up, supposedly unannounced at either 11 p.m. or 6:30 a.m. and put us through more rigorous exercises euphemistically called sweat parties. Now, remember, we were also students. I was majoring in engineering.

"That first four months of being a member of the Rat Mass, that purgatory of non-being, not even considered a fourth year—freshman—cadet.

"That wouldn't happen until Breakout, sometime in January, when the survivors among us were welcomed into the fellowship of the Corps.

"We lost some to physical and emotional stress. One kid collapsed and died after a ten-mile march. It was no one's fault. He had an unusual heart condition that's hard to detect beforehand.

"And all the while, I watched that girl."

Hi … I'm Gus.

I know. I'm Lauren.

"I turned into a beet. It was hard to talk. Everyone was so busy, even in Crozet Hall. Breakfast, lunch, dinner—as Rats we had to stare straight ahead as we ate. But there are ways. You see a roster of names. You see names posted on the barracks rooms where girls are assigned. And you wait.

"The Old Corps, the upper classmen, put us through many a sweat party over the next four months. And then it was January, Resurrection Week, that final passage, that final step in becoming a true member of the Corps.

"Somehow, in some way, Lauren Fletcher and I managed to sweat our way up the four levels of the barracks together during Breakout. We became fourth year cadets together. We were now Brother Rats."

"Where are you from, Lauren?"

We sat together that Saturday afternoon after Breakout and finally delved into each other's backgrounds.

"Dad's a sheriff here in Lexington. Mom's a teacher."

I couldn't take my eyes off her raven hair.

"So …"

"She's part Amerindian, if that's what you're asking."

That girl could read my mind. "I … uh … never meant…"

"I know what you meant, Gus."

shoes

She laughed. Bells tinkled in my brain, as she squeezed my arm.

"Ah, no, I meant, what do you want to do after…"

I waved my arm to encompass the Post.

"I want to travel. Asia, the Mideast. My counselor says I have a natural aptitude for Arabic. Maybe I can get a semester overseas."

"Sounds exciting—and dangerous."

"And you, farm boy?"

I looked up and pointed as a jet flashed overhead.

"I want to fly, Lauren."

Kristin held me as I cried.

Kristin

He had fallen asleep in her arms.

She wiped the remnants of tears from his face then did her best to gently move him into his sleeping bag.

Now she was exhausted. But sleeping wouldn't help.

The crescent moon cast faint shadows from leaf-thinned tree branches as she rose and walked toward the little outhouse not far to the left.

When she was finished, she opened the weather-worn door and stepped back outside.

What was that?

The lunar light had coalesced. Other campers?

One small, two large, they moved toward her then stopped about fifty yards away.

The smaller one … a child? … waved … no … beckoned her.

She didn't realize she was moving, walking toward that youthful hand.

She felt the gold locket, still in her pocket. She reached for it and held it tightly.

The small light intensified, clarified. It *was* a child, a small boy.

"Mama?"

"Are you lost, little boy?"

What's a child doing up here? Where did the other ones go?

He shook his head and held out his hand once more.

The locket jumped in her hand.

"Mama?"

His hand touched hers, and the nocturnal mountain vista faded away …

Now it was May 1892. Spring had come to the valley farms around Lexington and Buena Vista. She heard the clip-clop, clip-clop of horse hooves on the hardened ground in front of the little clapboard farm house she and her husband called home.

She didn't rise as the tall, elderly man knocked on the half-open, hand-hewn door. She said nothing as he entered and stood nervously before her seated figure.

"Words cannot express my sympathy, Lillian. My wife and I wanted you to have this. I … uh … took this after I finished my … uh … examination of..."

The old doctor was dressed in full waist coat and vest. He was not a farmer. He wasn't one of the coarsely-dressed, hard-working Dunkards living in the valley. The gold chain and fob of his pocket watch glistened in the reflected spring sunlight of the open doorway. His brougham driver waited outside, brushing down the dapple-gray horse.

She wasn't old, but six childbirths take something out of a woman. So does the death of a child. She stared at the gleaming object in the old man's outstretched hand: a gold locket.

She shook her head. Her husband wouldn't allow it. Jewelry was not acceptable in their faith.

"Please, ma'am, take it. Look."

He opened the locket. A child's lock of chestnut hair lay within.

She was devout. She was strong. But to refuse this?

Her hands closed around the gold-cased memento mori and she held it to her breast.

The doctor nodded. "God be with you."

He turned and left.

She sat facing the window, the rough, handmade rocker not moving.

"Wife, why is the door open?"

He was covered with sweat from the farm work that filled his life. His hands were coarse and strong.

She didn't answer. Her gaze was unwavering, fixed on the mountain beyond.

He saw the flash of light from the object pressed against her chest.

"Lillian, what do you have?"

Slowly she opened her hands. He saw the object and shook his head.

"You cannot, you must not keep this. It is against our faith. Give it to me, Lillian"

He reached for it.

He did not expect the sewing shears aimed at his chest.

He did not expect her words.

"You took him from me once before. Not again."

He backed away.

Kristin opened her eyes as she heard herself saying "You took him from me once before. Not again."

The boy was gone.

She stared at the moonlit locket then turned toward the shelter.

In the opening, one of the larger images stood over her father.

A blink and it was gone.

Kristin Belmont stepped into her sleeping bag, holding the locket against her chest.

Drum Roll

I slept well that night—until Kristin's muffled snores wakened me, her head turned sideways under the flap of her sleeping bag.

She had slept that way as a child.

The early morning dew allowed me to walk soundlessly to the john, then I headed over to the Punchbowl mini-lake and watched the mountain breeze ripple on its surface. In some strange way, in that spot, I felt at peace with my fate.

The dawn sky was a backdrop for the theater of my mind…

"We're only six weeks away from graduation, Gus."

"Wanna get married in our dress uniforms?"

"Ducks and dykes?"

"Yeah, we can cut the cake with our sabers and accidently kill each other when we jam cake-tipped sabers in each other's mouths."

Lauren and I had laughed uncontrollably as we tussled on the grass in that very spot.

April was warm that year and we were the only ones up on the mountain so we did what young lovers will always do, given the opportunity.

"What's that noise?"

"Probably some peeping tom mountain lion"

She giggled. She always did just before…

"No, I hear it, too—rustling grass."

"Too late to worry about that."

We both erupted then lay back.

"I wonder what that deer or bear thought."

"That he was missing out on the action, big guy."

"Hope it wasn't your father, the sheriff."

"Nah, he knows he's gonna be stuck with you as a son-in-law. 'Course, that doesn't mean he won't shoot you if you're mean to his little girl."

"You ain't so little, girl."

We tussled once more as the sun rose that Sunday morning. But I heard the rustling again. It wasn't mountain fauna.

"Come on, Gus, let's get dressed before the tourists arrive."

"We could put up a sign: Don't feed the bares."

"Dad, Dad, where'd you go?"

The movie ended.

I didn't want it to end.

My daughter's voice startled me. I shrugged and called back. "Over here, Kris."

I could hear her running.

"Why did you wander off like that? You could have been carried off by bears or wild cats or…"

"Or ghosts?"

She stared at me.

"Wanna hear more about me and Lauren Fletcher? I guess I was a bit tired last night. Must have been food poisoning. See, your old man really is mortal … uh … or should I say human?"

We sat down on the grass. Wet bottoms didn't bother us.

"Where do I begin?"

"Well, from what I remember, you and Lauren had survived

the Rat Mass and got through Breakout together."

"Okay, so our first year was filled with academics and military training. We learned how to handle weapons and continued with our daily routine. Lauren actually did get her chance to go overseas that summer and, according to her letters, had an exciting time in Morocco. The other cadets in her group were great—with one exception."

"Did you miss her?"

"What do you think, girl? Don't you miss your boyfriend?"

She blushed.

"Think your old man didn't know about that?"

"Uh … you said all the cadets with her were great, except one. What did she say?"

"There was this one guy who kept trying to hit on her. She did her best to go easy on him, but he didn't get the message. When she finally told him to buzz off, he got a bit aggressive, if you know what I mean, and she cold-cocked him."

"He tried to rape her? Isn't that a violation of the Honor Code?"

"Hmm, I suppose you could say he was trying to steal something from her, but that would be a stretch. More likely sexual harassment, but she didn't do anything because they weren't on the Post, and she didn't want to cause trouble for a classmate. Lauren was good hearted even though she could throw a mean punch."

"But she…"

She was shaking her head.

"I know, Kristin, I know. But you had to know Lauren. She was tough, but she was also a softie."

"How soft, Daddy dearest?" She grinned, as I turned red. Damn!

"Hmm, well, in any event, we went through our second year and she actually outranked me at one point. She got her Corporal's stripes before I did!"

"Did she command you to…?"

"Be serious, young lady, be serious!"

"Did you know the guy who tried to…?"

"No, and I wish I had. I begged Lauren to tell me but she wouldn't. She warned me not to do or say anything because it would get me in trouble. Too bad. If I had found out, he wouldn't have been able to hit on any girl again."

"Lauren really knew you, didn't she?"

I miss her so much.

"She was one amazing girl."

"What about the other kids, your roommates?"

"We had a really mixed bag. I remember that first introduction in our barracks."

Oh, man, we all gonna fit in heah?

"Denzil, Denzil Johnson, was from D.C. He later told us it was the norm for him to share a room with at least four younger brothers. He and I roomed together later and we both joined the Air Force. He's still in. I got an email from him just before you found the friend on my neck. He's getting his star at his next pro board. He'll be flying a desk at the Pentagon pretty soon."

"Pro board?"

"Promotion in rank. He was my best man when your mom and

I got hitched. Remember the wedding photos we showed you?"

"That's Uncle Denny? Wow! What else did he say? I haven't seen him since we moved here to Virginia."

"He asked about you. I emailed him a picture. He also wanted to know if I planned on going to our twenty-fifth class reunion."

I won't tell her it's this week. I don't want them to see me like this.

"What about the others?"

"Our room was Spartan bare, just an old-fashioned radiator along the wall."

Where's our beds?

"When Abe Saltzman asked that question, our Cadre gave an evil grin and said, 'Your hays are rolled up against the wall.'

"We didn't say anything until he had left."

Holy shit, we're sleeping on the floor!

"Abe was our New Yorker. We never quite understood why he was at VMI. He was super smart, had been accepted to every Ivy-league school in existence and his family had money up the yin-yang. Not to say that the rest of us were morons or destitute. Our high school GPAs and SAT scores were top notch, too. But, somehow, I always saw Abe as a constitutional lawyer or a Harvard professor.

"We asked him why VMI. He smiled and said it was a damned good school and he wanted a total challenge—the same reason we were all there.

"That pretty much said it for all of us."

"What happened to him?"

"After graduation, Abe did go to Harvard, got his law degree and clerked for the Supreme Court. He's an appellate court judge now. He was also the judge for Donny Ashburn's Honor Court trial."

"Did he have any doubts about the verdict?"

"No, Kris. None of us did."

Except Lauren

Did we make a mistake?

"Who were the other two in your room?"

"Ah, good old Toby Bessel was the tallest at six feet, two inches, a beanpole-thin, one-hundred-forty pounder who hailed from Richmond."

Guess this is what we signed on for, too, guys.

"He was friendly but shy."

"What fabulous things did he do later?"

"The greatest thing any cadet can do. He was killed in Afghanistan, trying to rescue one of the men in the unit he commanded. His name is forever engraved on the honor roll of VMI cadets who gave their all for their country."

"Oh … I'm sorry, Dad."

"So am I. He was one helluva guy, a true southern gentleman.

"Let's see, Denzil, Abe, Toby. Our fifth at the Mad Hatter's tea party was Monty, Montgomery Passelman the third. You could almost hear a bugle blow when you said his name. Sounds kinda like a Civil War general's name, doesn't it?"

"Was he rich like Abe?"

"No, but he was just as smart. Came from Georgia, if I remember correctly."

Hey, look at it as a never-ending campout, guys.

"Monty, well, no one ever quite knew if he was serious or not. He smiled a lot. He turned toward me, still smiling after making that introductory statement."

You're a farm boy, aren't you, Gus?

Yeah, Sherlock Holmes, how'd you know?

Your hands and your skin: you got sun spots on your neck and calluses that none of us have.

Uh … Monty, how do you know it ain't from him bein' friendly with his hand, if you get my drift.

"Even I laughed as the ebony-skinned Denzil's deep bass voice echoed in the room. Of course, I had to answer. It's a guy thing."

Hey, if you want to be good … no, great … at something you gotta practice a lot, right?

Yeah, Gus, just don't practice on me.

I don't think we need to worry about him. Did you see old Belmont here staring at that tall chick? If he coulda stepped outta formation, I think he woulda done some partner pushups with her.

"Toby was shy but had an observing eye."

Yeah, just call me Zeus.

"I told you it was a guy thing, daughter. But we did have partner pushups and sit-ups in calisthenics. Needless to say, that's not what the other guys meant. At that point we hit the showers and waited for our first sweat party. That night's soiree, compliments of our upper classmen cadre, left us too exhausted for anything except the sleep of the just."

"What happened to Monty?"

"He joined the Army and wound up in Army Intelligence. He and Denzil are the only two in our little group to make star rank.

"Guess your old man didn't do much with his life, eh, Kris?"

"You had me. Wasn't that enough?"

"Yeah, you were one handful, kiddo. Not only did I have to worry about you bringing home poisonous snakes and other critters, I had to worry about all those boys at our front door. But, somehow, by some miracle, I think you turned out pretty damned good."

She was smiling, but I could still see the innocence in her eyes. She had never been hurt, except when Sandy and I divorced.

"Remember what I asked you just before you graduated from high school, Kristin?"

"You said a lot of things, even as you were leaving me at the dorm my first day at William and Mary, but…"

"Oh, yeah, you said that college wasn't high school and I said 'duh!' But I know what you mean now, Dad."

Do you really?

"Well, that's what it was like at VMI, too. I had professors I couldn't get enough of and others I prayed would stand in front of the artillery as it went off. And I learned that it was all up to me. If I did something stupid, I would suffer the consequences. You wouldn't understand punishment marches and guard duty, Kristin, and I know you wouldn't have tolerated being confined to barracks on weekends as punishment."

"What did you do that was stupid?"

"My junior year, three of us guys were off-post, legitimately, but the car we were in broke down and we didn't make it back before taps at 11:30 pm on Sunday. By school rules, we were officially AWOL, absent without leave.

We were summoned to the Commandant's office and he grilled us on the rules and then asked why we were late. I told him our car broke down and he said that was no excuse. Then I said a cadet was never to leave another cadet in distress and we had to stay with our friend until we could get the car fixed."

"Did he buy that?"

"In a way. He confined us to barracks for the next weekend and had to write an explanatory paper. It worked. We didn't get rolled out—expelled."

"What about the rest of your Brother Rats?"

"It really wasn't until Breakout that I finally had a feel for who my classmates were, the ones you could rely on in a pinch and those you kept at a distance. We called them 'loose cannons.' I also learned that human nature is what it is, even in the highly disciplined atmosphere of a military school."

"Did you fight with any of your roommates?"

"Hell, yes! When you jam five human rats into a small maze and subject them to military and academic stress, it's natural for tempers to flare."

Damn it, Monty, quit snapping that elastic on your underwear. I've got an exam tomorrow!

"Snap, snap, snap. Monty got a kick out of pulling Saltzman's chain."

I said stop it or I'll…

Get those two apart before they kill each other!

"It took the three of us, Denzil, Toby and me, to pull Abe and Monty apart. They were like two stags locking horns all the time. I think Monty felt Abe was looking down on him because he was from Georgia, although the rest of us never felt that way."

"Did you guys stay together after that first year?"

"Remember what you did with your first roommate, Kristin?"

"Yeah, I couldn't wait to get to another room. Thank God, you and mom let me get an apartment off-campus for the last three years. And Renee has been a great roommate."

"Think about it, girl. We didn't have that option. It was barracks or nothing. But, we could change each year, and as we became upper classmen, we had the option of just one roommate. Denzil and I stayed together our second year Abe and Monty were at each other's throats so much that it was a relief to see them both switch off.

"Toby hooked up with one of the guys in the next room and Abe and Monty both found other roommates for second year. By senior year, one of the big privileges was having a single room for yourself."

I saw the look in her eyes.

"No, fraternization in your room with women cadets was not allowed. Lauren had her own room senior year, too."

"Okay, but what about camping out?"

"Lauren knew this area backwards and forwards. She grew up here. One weekend we both had off from Saturday afternoon through Sunday evening. It was springtime and she said she

chestnuts

wanted to show me some neat sites around Lexington.

"Next thing I know, I'm driving her friend's motorcycle with her on the back playing human GPS. Her mom had packed us a picnic basket and her dad, the sheriff, gave me the evil eye while smilingly telling me to keep his daughter safe."

Cadet Belmont.
    Yes, sir, Sheriff Fletcher?
    I expect you to be a gentleman at all times. Understand?
    Uh, yes sir.
    Daddy?
    Yes, Laurie?
    What if I don't want him to be a gentleman?
    Leave the young ones alone, Fletcher.
    Yes, mother.

"The sheriff always called his wife by that name. Lauren's parents were so much in love. I like to think she and I would have…"
    Oh, crap! I'm doing it again.
    "Come on, Dad, you haven't finished the story."
    "There were other times our first two years when the 3:30 a.m. knock on the door and the call of 'Your Honor Court requires your presence' sent us scurrying to the stoops of our rooms, wrapped in our blankets to keep us warm.

"The Honor Code is sacrosanct. A cadet will not lie, cheat, steal nor tolerate those who do. Those first two years I heard the names of eight cadets whose names would never be spoken again in barracks."

The snare drums roared in my ears. I had to stop.

"Dad...?"

"Yes...yes. Where was I?

"Okay, our second year was notable for the start of our 'camping' excursions. But there were a few sour notes. Other cadets tried to get friendly with Lauren, and some never took the hint, even when Lauren became blunt."

Fletcher?

Yes?

I ... uh ... wanted to know if you would like to accompany me to the Ring Figure?

"I was not more than five feet away when the other guy saw me. Lauren smiled politely."

I appreciate your offer, but I have other plans.

"His face turned the color of his guard sash."

You getting stuffed by Belmont, here, or are the guys at Washington and Lee more your type?

Don't answer him, Lauren.

What's the matter, Belmont? I'm asking you both a direct question. Are you two an item?

"We stood there, trying not to react. We didn't take the bait. Even though it would have been a stretch, the other guy might have tried to file an Honor Code violation against us both for lying."

"Dad, that's ridiculous!"

"Yes, but remember, human nature is what it is and some

cadets, fortunately just a few, tried to pervert the system for their own gain and petty control needs. Thank God the Honor Court doesn't fall for that stuff.

"Anyway, the guy was a loner at the Ring Figure."

"What's a Ring Figure?"

"It's a coming of age ceremony followed by a formal dance ball. Halfway through your third year, junior year, usually in November, the second classmen are formally presented with their class rings. We call them nuggets, because they're large, gold, and heavy. Then a formal dance is held. It's a gateway to your last year at VMI."

"Where's your nugget?"

"Funny you should ask."

I reached into my pocket. I hadn't worn it in ages. The class ring I usually wore was the stainless steel one, the practical second ring that cadets could wear without fear of losing while on hikes and such. The gold one, the nugget, was usually for ceremonial and festive occasions. Now the demon within me had made my fingers too thin to wear it properly.

I had planned to exchange rings with Lauren at our wedding.

"Here, Kris, it's yours now."

I stood up and pretended to stretch. My legs felt shaky. I had to sit down again but I faked it by sliding back on my rump.

"Daughter, you are looking at a full-fledged member of the Honor Court!"

"You mentioned the Ashburn thing, Dad. What was he like?"

"Don was one of the quiet ones; friendly, but not really a joiner or a self-starter. I got the impression that he could be swayed by the opinions of others. He did well in school, though, and that's what made the whole thing, the cheating episode, so strange."

"How did you and Lauren get to be on his jury? Did every cadet have to serve, like civil juries?"

"No, in our third year, the entire class elects representatives to the Court. It's a great honor because your peers select you. Both Lauren and I were nominated and both of us served through our last year and … and…"

The nausea overwhelmed me. I couldn't remain upright.

"Dad!"

I marched in darkness to the beat of the snare drum.

Predator

So many to choose from.

He was a first classman now, a senior. He had his own room. It was the first time he had slept alone.

"I could have had my own room, Pa. Our house was big enough."

He made sure that his fourth class student, a freshman, kept it clean.

It was nice having the perks of senior year.

Move your ass, boy. Clean this place up.

"Yes, Pa."

He looked in the mirror.

"You are definitely first class, old man."

He scowled, as the mirror reflected an image from his past: a short, thin boy child. It stared back at him.

"We weren't always so first class, were we?"

A voice erupted from the silvered glass.

You are one pathetic piece of shit.

"But, Pa, why did you hit me? You said you wanted me to clean the house."

You never do anything right, that's why.

"Why do you always hit me, Pa?"

Because I can, boy, because I can.

The image of his father's scornful face was forever burned in his memory.

"Nothing was ever good enough for you, Pa. How did it feel when I beat the shit out of you when I turned fifteen? Did I do that right?"

He smiled back at the mirror.

"They never did find your body. Yeah, Pa, you were right about one thing: it is fun to play with people's minds. But I won't make your mistake. They won't know I'm doing it."

He looked down from his stoop and saw the underclassmen.

Sheep—all sheep.

He was a planner, very thorough with assignments, very meticulous at drill and anything else military. He also loved to play chess—with human pawns.

He had that planned out, too: first a military career, then politics.

Just like you, Pa.

He shivered in orgasmic delight at the thought of all those human sheep under his future control. He laughed out loud as a new chess gambit came to mind.

Recipe: take one or two easily malleable sheep personalities. Add a convoluted scheme to convince them that they are doing something important for the school. Then watch, as they self-destruct.

Maybe even get rolled out.

He loved those 3:30 a.m. ceremonies.

His feral eyes scanned the student body in flux; a computer mind spotted its prey: *E pluribus one sucker.*

He'd intercept that one in barracks. The sheep was a senior, too.

As he turned, his eye caught sight of something less pleasing.

You're still hanging around Belmont, aren't you, Fletcher? I'm not good enough for you, eh?

He rubbed his jaw. Three years later, her sucker punch still stung.

He adjusted his uniform and stepped into the hallway.

"Hey, Ashburn, can I have a word with you?"

Prey

The saber glistened in the afternoon sunlight.

"This was mine, Donnie."

"Wow, Dad, your VMI saber!"

"You've got four hard years ahead of you. If you make the cut, it will be yours."

Matilda Ashburn smiled at the unlimited enthusiasm of the eighteen-year-old boy.

He's smart and strong, but…

"Donnie, are you sure this is what you want? You've been accepted at UVA and all those other schools. And …"

"Mattie, it's the boy's decision."

Thaddeus Ashburn had done well in both military and business. He was a self-starter, focused at all times. His only regret was not making it into the green berets like his twin brother Lon. But Lon was gone, killed in 'Nam, so he had to carry on.

"Mom, Dad, I'm sure. I want to be a Brother Rat like you, Dad."

The older man smiled but held the same thought his wife hadn't verbalized: Donnie was so trusting, so innocent.

"Hey, I'm gonna go into Lexington and tell Aunt Abby. Okay?"

They watched as the lean, blond-haired, hazel-eyed high-school track star ran out the door.

"How did he grow up so fast, Mattie?"

She looked at her six-feet-tall husband. "He's taller than you, Thad."

"Aunt Abby, Aunt Abby, I got accepted to VMI!"

He almost danced around the middle-aged woman who ran

the little antique shop near the business district in Lexington.

"That's wonderful, Donnie. Now, listen up, boy. I've heard the stories yer pa's told about the school. You do the best ye can, understand?"

"Yes, auntie."

"All right, now, don't forget to stop by and show me what ye look like in yer soldier outfit. Understand, boy?"

"Yes, ma'am."

She watched as he threw her a mock salute and raced out the door.

She dabbed at her eyes before turning away. He looked so much like someone else, someone who had left her almost nineteen years ago to fight in the fields of Southeast Asia.

He never returned.

"Hey, Ashburn, got a minute?"

"What's up?"

"I need some help with a Psych/Sociology project."

"Help? You know I can't do your project for you."

"No, no, it's not that type of help. Here, stop by my room this evening and I'll go over what it is, okay?"

"Okay."

"So, that's my outline. The school wants to see whether the Honor Code is truly relevant in today's Post culture. They want to see if fellow students truly believe in it and will turn in those who … you know…."

"So, you need a plant to do things against the code to test it? And the professors are all in on it?"

"Would I ask you if they weren't?"

"What do you want me to do?"

"Pretend to cheat on an exam."

Rollout

"Is he conscious?"

She stared up hopefully at the lanky rescue squad tech.

"No. He's in status."

"What's happening to my dad?"

"He's having seizures, Ms. Belmont."

The EMT from the county rescue squad was barely twenty two, but he had seen this before: cancer patient, brain metastasis, status epilepticus—non-stop convulsions. Not good. He didn't have the heart to tell her.

The young tech was inserting needles in Gus Belmont's forearm veins, while his partner was on the squawk box with the ER at University Hospital in Charlottesville. The ER doc was giving the first responders directions.

"Give him 5 milligrams diazepam and 4 milligrams dexamethasone IV. Let's see if that holds him. And guys, don't forget to get the number of his personal doctor from his daughter."

The first tech stretched his six-feet-two lanky frame after the IVs were started and the drugs given. Within seconds, the total body twitching had stopped.

"Ms. Belmont, we'll need you at the hospital for information … the usual stuff. You want to ride with us?"

Kristin Belmont was running on adrenalin. She shook her head.

"I … I'll follow you in our car."

It can't be happening this fast. Dad said six months. This can't be happening!

"Uh … I don't recommend that, Ms. Belmont. Tell you what. You ride with me, and then we'll come back later for your car.

Okay?"

His smile seemed genuine. Somehow it comforted her.

"Okay."

She sat in the back of the ambulance, her eyes not straying from her father. His body no longer shook. His skin was pale

The tall EMT, "call me Beau," held her hand.

Where the hell am I?

"He's seizing again!"

Beau grabbed the microphone as his partner navigated the circuitous mountain roads toward Charlottesville.

"Two more of diazepam and decadron," the radio blared back.

Am I dying?

No, Gus. You're being taken to the emergency room.

Who are you?

You know me, Gus.

Why can't I see you?

Not yet, Gus.

Why can't you give me a straight answer?

You'll know soon enough. Here, maybe this will help. Take a look.

The gray slowly cleared.

Is that me?

Yes.

Geez, I didn't know I looked that bad. That can't be me lying on that cart. And, by the way who or whatever you are, Voice, I'm no

*prude but I wish they'd throw a sheet over me. I don't want Kristin
to see me like that.*

She won't.

Why not?

Look over there.

He saw his daughter and a young man in rescue squad uniform
on the other side of the emergency room wall. He could see
through it. Kristin was crying.

*Come on, Gus, you've got work to do. Your Honor Court needs
you.*

Once more, the room dissolved into gray.

He ran down the barracks stairs, crossed the courtyard and exited
through the Washington Arch.

It was evening.

He crossed the two lane road and entered the building opposite.
Once more he ran, this time up five flights of stairs.

This can't be. I'm not even winded!

He opened the door without windows.

"Cadet Belmont."

"Yes, sir?"

"Please take your seat."

Four other cadets already sat at the long wooden table against
the right wall.

Holy shit, I'm back at school!

The windows were blacked out.

Flickering fluorescents cast shadow-free, blue-white light on the tile floor of the small classroom in Maury Brooke Hall.

He stared down at his hands. They were unwrinkled, the hands of youth. He moved them over the white ducks and gray shirt that covered a twenty-one-year-old body then looked at the others.

She was the fifth at the table. She turned slightly and a fleeting smile crossed her face.

Lauren!

Don't turn. Don't look at her!

Three years of discipline kept his eyes forward. But the trick he had learned as a Rat came in handy. Peripheral vision filled in her details.

The knock of a gavel directed his attention to a center desk.

"For the record, this session of the Honor Court is now official."

The presiding judge was his old roommate, Abe Saltzman. The prosecutor was a cadet he knew only in passing.

He saw the defendant sitting with his legal adviser at a similar table on the opposite side of the room. In the background were other cadets: witnesses for and against.

Saltzman cleared his throat.

"Cadet Donald Ashburn, you have been summoned before the Honor Court on a charge of violating the Honor Code of Virginia Military Institute. How do you plead?"

An older man, a civilian attorney, rose.

"Not guilty, Your Honor."

The judge nodded and the prosecutor stepped forward and faced the table of jurors.

"Cadet Ashburn is charged with violating the Honor Code. He was reported by his peers and professors for cheating on examinations and plagiarizing the work of others."

One by one, cadets were called forward, each noting specific times and places in which Ashburn was observed in the specified activities.

At each turn, the defendant's counsel scrutinized the testimony and questioned them.

"When was Cadet Ashburn notified of the charges?"

"Has there been any discussion among the jurors outside this courtroom regarding the defendant?"

"Is there any reason to believe that those filing the charges are doing so out of personal vendetta or maliciousness?"

It's a shame. He was a good cadet. It almost seems like he wants to be dismissed from school.

At last the arguments were finished. The judge turned toward the defendant's attorney.

"Do you have any additional questions or evidence?"

"Your honor, my client wishes to make a statement."

Ashburn stood but did not approach the witness chair.

"I was told that this was an experiment to test the Code process. I was told that the professors were aware of this test. I am not guilty of violating the Honor Code."

"Cadet Ashburn, who told you this? Is that person here to substantiate your statement?"

"No, your honor."

Saltzman sighed silently then turned toward the table of jurors.

shoes

"The jury will now deliberate."

Gus Belmont filed out with the four other members into an adjoining room. They weren't sequestered for long, even though Lauren kept raising Ashburn's final testimony. If what the cadet said was true, then….

The other four jurors, including Gus, countered with the lack of witness support. Besides, the prosecutor had done his homework. When the complaint was first made by the cadet's professor, the prosecutor had arranged for several other cadets to observe and report. The evidence was damning.

"Why didn't he name his witness," Lauren countered.

It didn't make sense.

They filed back into the courtroom.

The jury foreman handed the written verdict to the judge. He scanned it, nodded then looked toward the defendant's table.

The defense attorney rose and assisted the young man next to him to do likewise.

Abe Saltzman paused. This was the sixth case he had presided over since he had assumed the responsibility at the beginning of his senior year. He didn't like to do this to a fellow cadet, but the Honor Code was one of the reasons he had sought to become a student at VMI.

Without integrity, what separates us from the rest?

It was only a second but he had to steel himself.

"Cadet Donald Ashburn, you have been found guilty by a jury of your peers of violating the Honor Code. It is the decision of this Court that you be summarily dismissed."

He watched as his former classmate slumped back in his chair. Now the even harder part would begin.

Assuming the Commandant concurred, Ashburn would be removed from the Post.

Belmont and his fellow jurors felt the chill as well, as they heard the whispered "the Commandant concurs with the verdict."

Those in the courtroom watched as the disgraced cadet was led from the room by a special cadre. They heard the door to the stairway open and close and the quivering voice of Ashburn protesting his innocence as he was led down the five flights.

There would be a car waiting at the building entrance. Donald Ashburn's gear would already be loaded on it. Lights on low beam, the car would convey him to a motel room half-way between Lexington and Buena Vista, from which his family would take him home.

Gus didn't want to go down those stairs. He waited for Lauren, and they walked slowly down the front stairway together.

It wasn't over yet. There was still the 0330 procession led by the snare drummer into the barracks courtyard and the official Rollout ceremonial announcement.

Gus wondered if the drummer would cut another notch in his sticks. This would make six.

It was raining.

He hoped it would stop before Rollout.

Silently concealed in the shadows of darkness, another person had watched Ashburn loaded into the car and driven off.

The darkness concealed a smile.

"Donnie…"

The former cadet had just gotten back from dropping the letter in the motel manager's mail slot. He lay on the bed, his mind still not comprehending the events of the past three hours.

"Donnie."

The whispered voice was serpentine. He turned. "What are you doing here? Why weren't you there to testify for me? You promised!"

"I never said I would be there."

"Yes, you did."

"Come on, Donnie, you didn't really believe that story I told you, did you?"

"Go away!"

The other was taller, a shadow dressed in camouflage, wearing dark gloves and pullover cap.

"I had to see you. This completes my experiment. You know that, Donnie. I had to be sure that you didn't do anything … uh … stupid."

"Where were you? You promised to help me. You said the jury would understand after you testified that this was a special project that the professors knew about."

"Take it easy, Donnie."

"You said that the school was testing the effectiveness of the Honor Code."

"I said, take it easy!"

"No, I've got to clear my name. I'm going to the Commandant. I did this to help you."

"Uh … Donnie, I wouldn't do that."

He saw the look on the shadow's face. He saw him looking at what was on his bed.

"Put that down. That was my dad's ceremonial saber."

Donald Ashburn, former VMI cadet, stood up.

It seemed like the other person was moving in slow motion.

He felt the point of his father's saber touch a spot just above his navel.

He felt the sudden searing pain as it penetrated his shirt and then his skin.

Nausea overwhelmed him as it pierced loops of bowel and then came to rest in his abdominal aorta.

It was only a few seconds, but the boy could feel the gusher of blood fill his belly cavity.

The last words he heard were: "You shouldn't have threatened me, Donnie."

The other stared down at the body of his classmate. He carefully positioned Ashburn's hands in a grip around the top of the saber.

He looked around the room.

Nothing else to do. Good thing I wore gloves.

He wanted to whistle as he left the little motel room. He was too disciplined to do that. He was a planner. He knew what he wanted and how to get it.

It wasn't a long walk.

He managed to make it back in time for lights out.

Hell, I'll even make it to the stoop for Donnie's Rollout.

Only one more loose end to tie up before graduation.

shoes

Loose End

"He's still unconscious, Beau, but he's not seizing."

Jensen held the phone up between his ear and Kristin's, so she could hear what the hospital doc was saying.

I'm not unconscious! I can hear every damned word you say, quack!

He doesn't know that, Gus.

Ah, my invisible tour guide is back. Where to, now?

A time of happiness … and pain.

School, again, huh?

Come on, Gus.

It was cool that April. Not many weeks left to graduation.

"Wanna take a bike trip up to Bluff this weekend?"

"I can't, Gus. I promised my roommate I'd go with her to her parents' place in Richmond. We're leaving right after parade formation today."

"Darn, I wanted another chance to upset your father, Lauren."

"Come on, you know he likes you, even talks about you like a son. I think he's looking forward to us getting hitched after graduation."

"Yeah, sure. Why does he keep fingering his revolver whenever I'm with you?"

"Stop it. He really does like you. Besides, he never aims Old Betsy at anyone unless he's gonna shoot them."

"Now she tells me.

"Do your parents know you're gonna be away?"

She looked at the boy-man she loved so dearly and nodded.

"Hey, guys, did you hear? That kid killed himself!"

They were outside on the field getting ready for formation drill practice. It was a test run for graduation.

"What kid, Tim?"

"Ashburn."

Gus Belmont felt the air sucked out of him. He saw Lauren turn pale.

"No, Tim. We hadn't heard. That's awful."

Lauren had turned away.

He had to do something. He waited while the other cadet moved away then put his arm on her shoulder.

"We did our job, Lauren. It's not our fault. He had a fair trial."

"But he killed himself, Gus. Couldn't there have been another way?"

He wanted to hug her. He couldn't do it here. All he could do was repeat meaningless words.

They marched that early Saturday afternoon, their drill performance flawless. Some of the local parents sat in the bleachers and cheered them on. He knew Lauren's parents were there. They always showed up.

"Hey, Belmont, good job."

"Thanks, Sheriff Fletcher, Mrs. Fletcher."

"You gonna let my daughter go away for a day without giving her an argument, boy?"

"She's a big girl, sir."

"Dad, it's only until tomorrow. Come on!"

She was surprised when her father took her hand and then

Gus's hand and brought them together.

Sunlight glinted off their giant class rings, the nuggets they would wear and exchange at graduation.

"Listen, boy, you two have my blessing. Couldn't ask for a better guy for my little girl. But … don't forget, I'll always have Ol' Betsy … just in case. Understand?"

The big sheriff laughed, as he patted his holster.

Gus watched, as father and mother hugged their daughter. He wished school protocol would let him do that openly. It didn't.

"Okay, guys, see you tomorrow evening."

"Watch yourself, daughter."

I can't tell them. I gotta get away from here. Jesus, why did Ashburn have to go and kill himself?

She had to have alone time. At first it had been the building pressure of graduation. Now guilt weighed on her.

She changed out of her dress uniform then carefully removed the gold class ring and replaced it with the stainless steel one that seniors wore routinely.

Uh oh, it's getting loose. Must be losing too much weight. Stress? Gotta eat more.

Yeah, right, this close to graduation. Suck it up, girl. Get it resized later.

She snugged the ring as best she could.

It was an easy cross-country jog for her. She could beat the pants off any guy at running. Off the Post and a short distance outside Lexington, she found the car she kept hidden off the road.

Only Gus and her parents knew about it. It was her safety valve for the past three years, second best only to Gus.

She checked the back seat. The whiskey bottle was there, too. Not illegal—she was twenty one, after all—but on the Post? No way.

Her camping gear was safe, too.

Okay, chariot, take me away.

It wasn't too long before she was driving up to the parking area at the base of Bluff Mountain.

Another car remained a distance behind.

The hike from the lot to the camping site three quarters of the way up normally invigorated her at this time of year. Cool breezes, early spring plants poking their first green stalks above ground, some slight leafing out but mostly bare trees. It was the beginning of spring resurrection.

She loved this time of year. Life was recycling itself from a Stygian winter.

She trudged easily across the field, her feet crunching the dried out leaves and catkins from previous years, and arrived at the three-sided shelter. She removed her pack and headed to the outhouse. By that time sunset was a purple red haze, but still light enough to head back via the Punch Bowl pond before starting a campfire.

When she was a little girl she used to pretend the Punch Bowl was a giant crystal ball. She would giggle and laugh as her father and mother would tell ghost stories around the camp fire then pretend she could see the future in the moonlit watery surface.

She stood there a brief moment.

O great crystal ball, what will my life with Gus be like?

Nothing, not even a tree reflection.

Twenty minutes later, she had started her campfire in the fire pit just outside the hiker's shelter.

She munched on a granola bar and opened the Johnny Walker Black Label then took a swig.

Easy, girl, ya gotta hike down this mole hill in the morning. Don't go getting tipsy.

What the hell, why not?

By the time the three-quarter moon had risen, she felt a bit of a buzz. She started to climb into her sleeping bag when nature's call warned her to make another trip to the outhouse.

The buzz had dulled her senses. She didn't hear the rustling behind her until she heard the nearby breathing. As she turned, she felt a searing pain in her abdomen, followed by nausea and dizziness. Her hands reached down and felt the cold steel penetrating her skin and the swelling as blood filled her belly.

She couldn't understand why her ring had turned red.

Then, moonless darkness.

She didn't feel herself being dragged.

She didn't hear the muttering male voice.

"Didn't think I knew about that car, did you?"

He pulled the blade out with difficulty. It seemed stuck.

"Damn, the tip broke off in the bitch. I can grind it down so no one will notice."

She didn't see or hear him dig the hole. She didn't feel the cold dampness, as her body was flung into it. She didn't feel her ring slip off her now limp finger and fall to the top edge of the pit she now lay in. The pounds of mountain soil, rock, and forest debris that covered her caused no pain.

He was a careful man, a planner. His training had taught him the art of concealment. He made sure to make the site indistinguishable from the surrounding field.

He took her camping gear and trudged back down the mountain. It would be easy to dispose of. The broken saber? That would get turned into the Armory before graduation. Once he refinished the tip, no one would know the difference.

He didn't see the small luminescence hovering over the now-concealed grave.

He didn't see a larger light rise from that site and join the lesser one.

He hummed quietly to himself as he made his way down the mountain.

How's it feel now, Fletcher? I was never good enough for you, was I? Who's good enough for you now?

Say hello to my pa, bitch.

"Where's Lauren?"

"Isn't she with you, Gus? We thought she returned to barracks on Sunday."

Mrs. Fletcher heard the worry in the boy's voice.

"Did you check with her roommate?"

"She never went with her."

He stood with Lauren's parents in the Commandant's office on Tuesday.

Search parties fanned out across the Post and up into the mountains. The car registered in her name was found in the parking lot at the bottom of the mountain ridge.

After one week and three days of heavy April rains that turned to snow up on the mountain peaks, the search was called off.

Next

Abigail Mayhugh slid off her chair.

"Damn, I hope she hasn't had a stroke or an MI."

Beau Jensen quickly knelt down next to the shop owner and began checking her vital signs.

The old woman's eyes rolled up in her head, and her body twitched a few times, before she lay still again. Her eye lids fluttered then opened.

"What … what …?"

"Vagal reaction. Nothing serious."

Kristin and Beau had left the hospital after the ICU doctor had given the word: "He's stabilized for now, Ms. Belmont. Why don't you get some rest?"

Beau turned toward the exhausted girl. "I'm off duty now. Let me take you over to your car and then I'll show you some of the local motels where you can stay."

"Thanks, Beau. Uh … is that really your name?"

"Yep, it's Beau, Beau Jensen. What's yours?"

"Kristin."

She didn't want to stay in Charlottesville. It wasn't that far a drive. She had to do something. A small motel just outside Lexington would serve as a pit stop. It just seemed like there was unfinished business there.

"You sure you don't want to stay in Charlottesville? You really should rest."

The young EMT had seen this before—the need to do something, the agitation of having to face a loved one's mortality.

"I've got to talk to someone Dad and I met while we were in Lexington, Beau."

There are too many loose ends. Something doesn't fit. First, that woman in the antique shop and her nephew that Dad helped judge guilty at VMI; then the locket and that kid up on the mountain. Maybe I'm going crazy, but I need answers.

"Mind if I come with you?"

She looked up at him, smiled, and nodded.

He followed her down the mountain into Lexington. They parked their cars together.

The little antique shop was open. Beau held the paint-peeled door, barely sidestepping as the girl rushed through it into the darkened anteroom.

"Mrs. Ashburn?"

"That was my twin sister Mattie's married name, girl. She's dead. I'm Abigail Mayhugh."

"Oh, sorry, Mrs. Mayhugh."

"It's Miss, and I don't take returns, girl."

The old woman was sitting in the same chair as before. It didn't look like she had changed her dress either. She stared up at the girl and saw the young man standing next to her.

Hmpfh, probably the boyfriend. Looka him sniffin' aroun' her.

"Oh, no, Miss … uh … Mayhugh, I really love the locket. It's just that, well, I was wondering if you know anything about it … you know … where it came from, who owned it, that sort of thing."

"It ain't stole, if that's what you mean."

"Try being civil for once, Miss Mayhugh. Yeah, I remember you chasin' me away when I was a kid. I'm Beau Jensen. My dad owns this building. Understand?"

The old woman started to tremble at the boy's steady blue-eyed stare.

"I … I meant no disrespect, girl. It's jes…"

"No, no, don't be upset, Miss Mayhugh. It's … well … you said you couldn't open the locket. That's why you sold it so cheaply"

"And…?"

"I opened it."

Abigail's face matched the color of her gray dress. She started to rise then fell back in her chair.

Between her sobs, the two young ones could make out only one word: "Ottie." Then her eyes rolled up and she slid off her chair.

Jensen stood up, brushed the dust from his jeans, and cast a side-glance at Kristin. Then he bent over once more and easily lifted Abigail back into her chair. He pulled two musty velvet side chairs over, brushed the dirt off their cushions, and waved Kristin to sit down in one while he took the other.

Kristin stared long and hard at the woman.

"Miss Mayhugh, I want some answers. What's the story on this locket?"

Abigail twisted the faded lavender handkerchief in her hands. She couldn't avoid the hard looks from the young woman or the Jensen boy.

"Girl, do you know about the little boy on Bluff Mountain?"

"Ottie Cline Powell, the little boy who wandered off and died on the mountain over a century ago? Yes, my dad told me about him. We saw the marker at the summit."

The old woman paused. How much should she tell them?

"My great grandpa was one a' the ones who searched fer the Powell boy when he wandered off. Grandpa t'weren't much older than the boy at the time.

He tole us kids how Ottie went missin' fer months, 'til hunters found his body up on Bluff.

When the doctor examined his body, he did an…"

"Autopsy?" Jensen interjected.

She nodded.

"Well, the story goes the doctor took a lock of the child's hair, put it in a gold locket and gave it to Ottie's mama. Her husband didn't want her to keep it. Somethin' about their religion and not having jewelry; stuff like that."

"How could he be so cruel?" Kristin was upset. The words "You took him from me once…" echoed in her mind.

"He weren't cruel, girl. He was a minister and his faith required it. But his wife wouldn't let him take it away from her. She held that locket to her dyin' day. She wanted to be buried with it."

Mayhugh was out of breath. She stopped and stared at the gold trinket in Kristin's hands.

"Now, remember, I can't say iffin it's true or not, but Grandpa said when Mrs. Powell was laid out, someone removed the locket before the coffin was closed. Some say it were the husband, but no one knows fer sure. Anyways, the locket was found among some stuff that got sold after a neighbor died years later."

"How did you get it?"

Kristin's hazel-blue eyes wouldn't let the old woman go.

"It were one o' the first things I bought when I opened my shop. It's been here over forty years. No one wanted to buy it … until you and yer pa came along. I thought I was done with it."

Her curiosity overcame fear.

"Did ya really open it?"

"Yes, ma'am."

"Did it have a lock a' the boy's hair?"

Kristin nodded.

"Ah." She hesitated. "It really should be with his mama."

"Where is she buried, ma'am?"

Beau saw the look on Kristin's face. There was no turning back. He rose and Kristin started to do the same then stopped.

"Miss Mayhugh, when my dad and I came in that first time, you were pretty rude to him."

Beau sat down again. *Geez, what is it with women?*

Abigail saw the girl's involuntary hand motion to her neck and the object hanging from a chain down the open part of her pale blue blouse: a ring, a heavy gold ring.

"Where's yer pa, girl?"

"Her dad's in the hospital, Miss Mayhugh. Remember what I said about being civil?" Beau's frustration tolerance wasn't high.

Damn, it's turning into a cat fight.

"I tol' ya. My nephew, little Donnie, they kicked him outta that college yer Dad went to. Said he violated their Honor Code. Poor boy. His mama gave me his letter jes' before she died. He wrote to her. T'wasn't his fault. It was someone else."

"May I see that letter?"

"He's dead. My boy's dead!"

"Your boy?"

Kristin was stunned. She finally understood. She saw the confused look on Beau's face as she rose to put her arm around the other woman.

"Donnie Ashburn…he was your son, wasn't he?"

Abigail bent forward and pressed her hands against her face.

"Donnie, my Donnie…he didn' have t' die. He shoulda tol' the school."

"Your sister raised him, didn't she? You weren't married and…"

The old woman could just shake her head and sob.

Kristin's soft voice was barely audible. "May I see his letter?"

She helped Abigail to stand. The old woman tottered then went toward an old fold-down oak desk and pulled up the cover. Disturbed dust floated in the air. She reached for a black leather holder, untied the string and pulled out an envelope bearing the VMI return address on the left upper corner. Beneath it was hand printed a name: Cadet Donald Ashburn. She held out the letter and Kristin gently took it from her hand.

"Miss Mayhugh, this letter … have you read it?"

"My boy's last words."

Kristin carefully peeled the upper flap of the resealed envelope back. The glue was powder dry, so it wasn't difficult.

"Beau, look at this!"

Together, the two young adults read down the scrawled,

obviously stress-filled handwriting.

"These aren't the words of a suicidal person, Kristin. This kid was determined to prove his innocence."

Beau had seen enough suicide notes working the rescue squad job.

"Ma'am, were the police sure that Donnie killed himself?"

"They tol' us he had used his father's saber—my sister's husband was a VMI graduate—to commit hara-kiri."

Kristin was the history major. "He stabbed himself to death with a saber?"

Abigail nodded.

"Why didn't you show this letter to the authorities?"

One look from the older woman and the younger woman knew the answer.

Kristin put her hand on Abigail's shoulder.

"Did Donnie know?"

Abigail shook her head. The memory of her boy rushing into her shop and yelling "Aunt Abby, I got accepted to VMI!" echoed in her mind.

"Miss Mayhugh, I want to look into this. I think you're right. I think Donnie was innocent. He may also have been murdered. May I borrow this letter?"

Abigail looked into Kristin's eyes.

So young, so innocent—like my Donnie.

Ma, give it to her!

Donnie?

She's the one, ma. She's my only chance to clear my name."

Abigail's shoulders straightened. She reached into another cubbyhole in the desk and took out a small jewelry box. She took Kristin's hand and placed it in her palm.

Kristin opened the box. It was another VMI ring, just as large as her father's and with the same date of graduation.

"It was Donnie's. He never had the chance to wear it."

"I … I can't take this, Miss Mayhugh."

"Please, girl. Clear my Donnie's name."

The Hunt

"Kristin, calm down!"

"I can't, Beau. I've got too much to do and so little time, I…"

She started to cry.

He held her.

It works for Dad when Mom goes off.

"I don't know what to do. Dad's dying. There's something in his past that needs closure. Damn it, after Abigail, I need closure!"

She wiped her eyes and stepped back.

"He watched the five-foot-six dynamo pacing back and forth on the sidewalk in front of the little antique shop in Lexington.

God, she's hot when she gets angry.

"Don't you see, something terribly wrong happened twenty five years ago. You didn't see my father's face when the Mayhugh woman first mentioned her son's name. The guy was even in his class. And Dad said his other classmate, Lauren Fletcher, disappeared just before graduation."

"Kristin, you said it was twenty-five years ago. Don't they have a class reunion coming up?"

"That's brilliant, Beau! Uncle Denny, my Dad's roommate, mentioned something about a reunion."

She pulled his head down and kissed his cheek.

"Uh … yeah … uh."

The kid who handled blood and guts routinely was now totally flummoxed. His face burned. He could barely keep his hand from rubbing the spot she had kissed.

Whoa, boy, you never had a kiss do that! Don't look down, don't look down!

"And we can check the morgue files at the *Lexington News Gazette*. I'm sure they've got all their stuff on computer now. They've been around here over two hundred years, so twenty-five is just a drop in the bucket for them.

"Beau, let's head up to VMI, first and check in at the alumni office."

"Uh, I can't do it right now. I gotta get back to school."

"School?"

"Yeah, I just work the emergency squad part time to make some extra money. I'm finishing up my senior year at UVA."

"Oh. Uh … what are you studying?

"I start med school next fall."

"Wow, that's neat!"

"Listen, Kristin, I'll help all I can. It's just … I got a class this afternoon then I'll have some free time. I'll stop by the newspaper and check the records on Ashburn and Fletcher for you.

I think it would also be a good idea to talk to Fletcher's father, if he's still alive. I remember my dad telling me that the old guy was in a nursing home."

"Okay, you get to class. I'll head up the hill to VMI. Do you have my number?"

Two cell phones were whipped out and numbers punched into memory.

Beau watched as the girl he had known for only twenty-four hours ran to her car and drove off.

Damn, you're falling for her, aren't you?

She knew the way now: through Lexington to the VMI sign, a right turn and a curling drive up to the top of the hill where the old Arsenal once stood.

Now the tawny buildings and castle-like Barracks confronted her.

It can't be this easy.

She saw the WELCOME ALUMNI sign in front of a building labeled Moody Hall. She parked in a small lot and hurried up through the open doorway. A woman with a sheath of computer printouts was headed toward her.

"Ma'am, can you help me?"

"I'm Carole Green. What can I do for you?"

"It's my father. His class is having its twenty-fifth reunion this year and…." Her energy evaporated. All she could do was stare at the other woman's name tag: DIRECTOR OF ALUMNI ACTIVITIES.

"What's your father's name?"

She could see that the young woman was tired.

"Augustus Belmont."

"Let's sit down. I think you're in luck. Twenty-fifth reunions are held in the fall. Let me see. It's this Saturday. I have a meeting with the class reunion chairman in just a few minutes. Did your dad register?"

Kristin gazed at the floor. "He's in the ICU at University Hospital in Charlottesville."

"Oh, I'm so sorry. What happened?"

"He's dying … cancer."

Green put her arm on Kristin's shoulder. "How can I help you?"

"Ms. Green, something terrible happened in my Dad's senior year. His classmate, Lauren Fletcher, the girl he would have married after graduation, suddenly disappeared that April and…."

"Yes, go on, dear."

"I don't know how to put this, but another classmate, Donald Ashburn, was drummed out on an honor code violation several days before Lauren disappeared. He supposedly killed himself in the motel room where he was dropped off after Rollout."

The director's skin started to crawl. She had heard about both the disappearance and the suicide. It was legendary at the school.

"Miss Belmont, what can I…?"

"Ms. Green, I have a letter the boy sent to his mother that final night. It implicates another cadet as the real culprit. It isn't the letter of a suicide-driven person. Besides, the missing cadet, Lauren Fletcher, served on the jury that convicted him."

She looked down once more.

"So did my father."

"Kristin, I think we'd better go to the Commandant's office. I'd also like the class representative to come with us. He's due any minute. Do you have that letter with you?"

"Yes."

He couldn't wait for the embryology class to finish. It was still daylight, so he headed over to Lexington once more and stopped by the offices of the Gazette.

"Hey, Jensen, got any scoops on accident victims?"

"Come on, Jake, you know I couldn't tell you if I did."

"What's up, kid?"

Jake Williams had seen a lot in his day. His gray hair was testimony to the more harrowing stuff. He had quit smoking at his wife's insistence five years ago, but Beau could see and hear the incipient lung pattern of COPD—chronic obstructive pulmonary disease—in his fruity cough.

"Need some info on the months of March and April for the year…"

"That's twenty-five years ago, boy."

"Yep. By the way, remember old Sheriff Fletcher?"

"Boom-boom Fletcher? God, yes. I can still see him pointing that big .45 revolver at a perp when I was a cub reporter here."

"Is he still around?"

The older man nodded.

"Poor guy. His daughter went missing from VMI a month before she was going to graduate. They never found her. His wife pined away and died a year later, and he just withdrew. I heard he had a stroke a few years ago. I think he's in the independent living section of the Mayflower now."

The old reporter was no fool.

"Beau, this got anythin' to do with the sheriff's daughter?"

The younger man grabbed a chair and straddled it.

"You believe in Fate or Karma, Jake?"

"Dunno, kid. I've seen a lot o' crap in 'Nam. Some guys lived and shouldn't have. Other guys died. Made no sense who made it and who didn't."

"Yeah, well, I met this girl and…"

"You in heat, boy?"

Beau turned beet red. "No, no, come on, now, Jake, let me finish."

Heh-heh, I know the signs boy. Can't hide it from ol' Jake.

"Well, we had to get this guy off the top of Bluff Mountain. He's got cancer and he started convulsing right in front of his daughter and I got to meet her and…."

"Whoa, Beau, so far all you've said is 'girl.'"

"Yeah, well, turns out her dad and the Fletcher girl were an item back in the day at VMI. Lauren Fletcher would probably have been this kid's mother if she hadn't disappeared.

"But here's the kicker, Jake. Another cadet killed himself in a motel right after he was drummed out. Both this girl's dad and the Fletcher girl were on his Honor Court jury."

Jake's forehead creased.

"Geez, boy, I was the reporter with Sheriff Fletcher that night. Weren't pretty, the kid lyin' on the floor with his dad's ceremonial saber stuck in his guts and blood all over that room. I can still smell it, know what I mean?"

An EMT knew that smell, too.

"That's what I mean, Jake. I can't tell you the whole story yet, but this girl—she's damned smart and good looking, by the way—got hold of a letter the Ashburn boy mailed shortly after he was deposited at the motel. It doesn't fit."

"I felt the same way, too. The look on that kid's face: it was surprise. I never seen that with any other suicides and I seen plenty. It's a college town, after all."

The reporter's face took on a look Beau had seen before: cunning.

"Listen, kid, I'll help ya, but ya gotta promise you'll call me if anything breaks, okay?"

"Agreed. Now, can you let me at those files?"

"Sure. Hey, I hear you're goin' to med school next year. How come you ain't joinin' yer dad in the real estate business? He must own half the county by now."

"I guess I don't have the smarts for it, Jake. No doubt I'm a disappointment to him. From the time I was twelve I wanted to hound-dog old Doc Shepland around instead of working in Dad's office."

"Yeah, I heard about that, too, kid. Shepland says you remind him of himself. Did ya know he worked as an ambulance driver back when he was younger than you? Apparently some young doctor he met while workin' the ER run down in Richmond got him hooked on med school."

"Was it Doc Galen?"

"Yeah, that's it. Hey, kid you gonna treat old Jake if I get sick?"

"You won't need me if you stay off the cigarettes, Jake."

"You sound like my wife, boy."

They laughed, two men, one aging, one just beginning, but neither understanding women or life.

Beau left an hour later with a handful of printouts and a smile on his face.

Crescendo

"You realize what you're saying, Miss Belmont?"

Three people sat in the Commandant's office. The fourth remained standing.

"Yes, sir, I do. I think that Donald Ashburn was set up. I think that whoever set him up also murdered him. He did a good job of making it look like suicide. But please let me be very clear. I do not fault the Honor Code and the Honor Court. They came to an honest judgment based on the evidence they had."

"Judge Saltzman?"

The class reunion chairman cleared his throat.

"Sir, I remember Miss Belmont's father. Gus was a fine cadet, and I'm proud to call him a Brother Rat. I also remember Ashburn and Fletcher. Don was a quiet kid, and all of us were surprised that he was brought up on honor code violations. It didn't fit him.

"As for Lauren, we all expected her to be our class's first general. Most of us suspected foul play when she disappeared."

The Commandant stared at the letter lying on his desk. He picked up the envelope. The postmark was dated the day Ashburn was found dead in the motel room.

"Abe is there anyone on your class roster that you…."

He couldn't say the words.

Saltzman stared back and nodded.

"There was one guy. The rest of us thought he was a prick … uh … I'm sorry, Miss Belmont, Ms. Green … I don't mean to be vulgar. And, strange to say, Ashburn was the only cadet who could tolerate him."

"Who?"

Appellate Court Judge Abraham Saltzman stood up, stepped toward the Commandant's desk, held up the class roster and pointed at a name. The Commandant glanced at it then held the hand-written letter up once more.

"Sweet Jesus!"

Just then, Kristin's cell phone started to vibrate.

"I'm sorry, would you excuse me a moment? This may be the hospital calling about Dad."

The other three nodded, as she stepped out of the room.

"Kris, it's me, Beau."

She noted the familiarity.

"Thank God. You can't believe what's happening."

"Same here. I think we need to visit the sheriff. Are you done there yet?"

"I will be. Have you heard anything about Dad?"

"Yeah, no change. We'll stop by the hospital after seeing Fletcher. Okay?"

"I'll meet you in front of the antique shop."

"See ya."

She stepped back into the Commandant's office. The other three looked glum.

"Everything okay, Miss Belmont?"

"Yes, sir."

"Miss Belmont, nothing like this has ever happened before. There's no precedent in the entire history of VMI."

"If I may make a suggestion," Carole Green said, gazing at Kristin.

The Commandant nodded.

"I have a friend at FBI headquarters in Richmond. Let me call her and ask what can be done. If you are right, the statute of limitations never runs out on murder or abduction cases."

"She always comes up with an answer," the Commandant interjected. "Miss Belmont, may I make a copy of this letter and envelope?"

"Yes, sir. I promised Donald's mother I would return it."

"I thought she had passed on several years ago."

"Uh … it's a long story. I can't tell you now, but I will."

She stood up and took back the original letter after a copy had been made. She shook hands with the others in the room and then left.

Saltzman looked at Greene and the Commandant.

"That girl would have made one helluva cadet."

She saw the blue-jeaned beanpole pacing back and forth in front of the little store.

He's got a nice butt.

By the time he had walked over to her car, she was laughing uncontrollably.

"What's with you?"

"Oh, nothing, Beau. What have you got?"

"I was lucky. Old Jake was on duty at the paper. He was the reporter on call when the sheriff found Ashburn. He thought it didn't look like a suicide."

"Where's Sheriff Fletcher?"

"Move over, I'll drive. It's an independent and assisted living facility not too far from here."

Fifteen minutes later, they pulled into the parking lot of the little retirement village outside Lexington. The sun was an hour away from setting. They introduced themselves to the LPN in charge and were given directions to the third, chalet-sized cottage down from the administration building.

A knock on the door brought a gravelly, slightly distorted voice.

"It's late, dammit, but come in. Can't leave an old man alone, can you?"

Beau hesitated then turned the knob and slowly opened the door.

Two wall sconces illuminated a small anteroom. It held only a medium-sized, flat-screen TV. Several bench-like chairs rested against cream-colored walls and those had self-assist bars on either side. The generic, tan-brown rug, designed not to show dirt, showed wheel marks.

"Well, why are you disturbing my peace and quiet? I don't need any medicine and I don't want to participate in any group activities. In other words, leave me alone. Understand what I mean?"

A jowly, white-haired old man sat in a wheel chair to the side of the room. His ruddy face showed the effects of countless days outside in the elements. Powerful arms covered by a blue-flannel, long-sleeved shirt gripped the wheelchair rims and propelled it toward the two visitors.

Watery blue eyes squinted up at Kris and Beau.

"Damned if you both don't look familiar. Are you the Jensen boy?"

"Yes, sir. My dad told me how you used to chase him and his

friends when they tried to … uh … liberate some apples from a neighbor's tree."

The old man's crooked smile was friendly. The memories crossing his mind were almost visible.

"You, girl, I can't place ye, but still there's somethin' familiar 'bout yer face."

"I'm Kristin Belmont, Gus Belmont's daughter."

The old man's right hand rose involuntarily then dropped back to the armrest. He started to moan, his words unintelligible save for one: Lauren.

Kristin moved forward and knelt by his side.

"Please, no, Mr. Fletcher, please. We need to talk with you. We need your help."

Two sets of blue eyes met.

"Can't help ye, girl. Look at me. I ain't no good to nobody."

Jensen knelt down on the other side of the old man's wheelchair.

"You'll always be Sheriff Fletcher to me, sir. Please, listen to what Kristin has to say. It's about Lauren and something that may be related to her disappearance."

The old man's shaking stopped as the discipline of decades took hold.

"Speak yer piece, girl."

As she spoke, Beau noted the change in the old man's face. Gone was the sagging apathy. A lawman's mind was now in charge.

"I remember the Ashburn case. It never seemed right to me, either. That reporter, Jake Williams, thought so, too. But we was overruled by the coroner. And then, when my little girl went missing two days later...."

He tried to hide his face as tears came down the side unaffected by stroke.

Kristin took a handkerchief from her purse and wiped the old man's face.

He looked at her and smiled.

"You're jes' like yer pa, girl. Where is he now?"

He started to cry again when Kristin told him.

"Sheriff, look at the letter Kristin has. Did you know about this back then?"

Beau held the letter, while Kristin went to get Fletcher's reading glasses from a nearby table. The man's lips moved as he read the hand-scrawled words of a dead boy.

"Mother of Jesus, where did ye get this? We never saw this. It woulda changed everything."

An hour later, Beau could see the fatigue signs on Fletcher's face and hear the increased slurring of words.

"I think it's best to let you rest now, Sheriff. May we come back tomorrow?"

He nodded, and they turned to leave but looked back as the old man called out, "Come here, Kristin."

She followed him, as he wheeled himself into a small bedroom. There, on a bedside table, sat a small mahogany box. His hand shook, as he took it and placed it on his lap to open it.

"This was my daughter's. It was in her room when we came to take her stuff home."

shoes

His left hand reached out and took Kristin's left hand. His right hand dropped a heavy object into it.

She looked down on a gold class ring—Lauren's nugget.

Fletcher's eyes watered as he looked up at her.

"You might have been my granddaughter."

What Once Was Lost

"You need to get some Zs, Kris. You're running on empty."

She dropped him off at his car and promised to get some sleep at the motel he had shown her earlier. As he drove off, she waited until his car was out of sight then headed toward Buena Vista and the stretch of road leading to Bluff Mountain.

The amber-red glow of sunset cast final shadows over the valley and the town of Lexington below as she made the turnoff.

She had to stop suddenly.

PARKWAY CLOSED FOR THE NIGHT

No, no damned sign is going to stop me now!

She parked the car by the side of the road, hitched her camping gear on her shoulders and began to hike. It was longer than she had anticipated. She was out of breath by the time she reached the chained off section blocking the car route to the mountain summit.

She was moving on autopilot now. It was dark but she had a small LED flashlight. It kept her from tripping over the more obvious branches and rocks as she crossed the field to the hiker's shelter.

Ah, good, no one else here.

The chill air reminded her to throw some nearby kindling into the fire pit and light a fire.

She wanted to sleep but couldn't get her mind to shut down.

Dad. Donnie Ashburn. Abigail Mayhugh. Lauren Fletcher. Sheriff Fletcher. The names kept spinning around in her brain.

Her hand went to the ring she now wore on a chain around her neck.

Dad, what have we started?

The pocket of her blouse trembled. She reached toward it and pulled out the other two class rings: Lauren's and Ashburn's.

What happened, what happened to you?

Mama? Mama?

The little fire that had started to ember now suddenly flared up into a column of flame.

What the hell, the fire's moving toward me!

A will-o'-the-wisp glow, no more than three feet high, extended itself toward her.

She felt her hand tingle.

Why am I not afraid?

Mama? Mama? Where's Mama? I can't find her. Can you help me?

Ottie, can you help me?

The flame nodded.

Come.

She rose. An errant thought made her chuckle.

And a little child shall lead you.

Are you really Ottie, the little boy of the mountain?

The light flickered briefly.

They moved together, the sound of only one pair of footsteps disturbing the mountain quiet as they moved down and around, to the far end of the Punch Bowl. The pond came into view and the light stopped.

Another will-o'-the-wisp, this time taller, almost defined but still hiding at the edge of her imagination, rose like a gas flame.

It flickered, beckoning her to come forward.

Kristin froze. Her hand clutched at the rings and the light intensified.

Soon she was able to move. She walked slowly toward the glow until she was no more than three feet away.

Is that a woman's face?

The light wavered then slowly began to sink into the ground.

A cloud moved over the dappled moonlit sky then passed.

Kristin stood on the spot and dropped to her knees. She couldn't help herself. Her hands moved over the ground, pushing layered years of forest debris and decay away. How long she did it, she couldn't tell.

Then something hard scraped her hand.

She cracked a fingernail trying to pry it out.

It was encrusted with dirt. It was too heavy for a small stone.

She turned on the little LED flashlight she had brought along and tried to brush away what was concealing the heavy object. The light's purple-blue glow finally reflected off metal: a stainless steel class ring.

She flipped her cell phone and pressed the auto dial.

A sleepy young man's voice answered.

"Jensen. Who's calling?"

"Beau, I found her!"

Dies Irae

"Get the ground radar over here!"

She was wrapped in a blanket. She had sat there, not moving from that hallowed ground, until she heard the voices and saw the bobbing flashlights coming toward her. Now Beau hovered over her, checking for signs of hypothermia.

"She's okay, guys."

Jake Williams and a staff photographer came over.

"You're Miss Kristin Belmont?"

She nodded. She was too tired to speak.

Flashes went off in her face.

"Hey, guys, leave her alone for awhile."

Williams smiled at Beau.

Now tell me you ain't smitten by the dame, kid.

"We're getting a reading! There's metal down there, too."

The sound of shovels and gentle hand digging were lullaby to the girl. She leaned against Beau, now sitting protectively beside her, and closed her eyes. It would only be for a moment.

"There's bones—human!"

The shout startled her awake.

"Let the FBI forensics team handle it. Are they here yet?"

Helicopter blades whooshed through the night air.

"They're gonna have to land in the field. Give 'em a yell."

She stumbled, as she tried to get to her feet.

He caught her. She was like a feather in his arms.

"I want to see her! Let me go over there, Beau."

More footsteps: Men and women in dark jackets with FBI

emblazoned on the backs, carrying lab kits.

"It's all yours."

"Know who it is?"

Kristin moved unsteadily toward them, light reflecting off the ring she held in her outstretched right hand.

"It's Lauren Fletcher."

Then she collapsed.

"You're gonna be okay, Kris."

She opened her eyes. Her hands felt smooth linen sheets over her body. Peering down at her was a worried young male face.

"Where…?"

Her mouth was dry. So was her tongue.

He pressed the up button on the hospital bed and she felt herself sitting upright. He held a glass of water to her lips.

"Easy, take it slow. Sip it, don't gulp it."

It felt good going down. The roof of her mouth no longer felt like dried glue. She looked at him and tried to smile.

"Who ya callin' Kris, big boy?"

He bent over and kissed her forehead.

"Where am I, Beau?"

"University Hospital. You kinda crashed up there on ol' Bluff.

"Did they…?"

"FBI's got the remains at the state forensics lab at the Chief Medical Examiner's office in Richmond. The bones are definitely young adult female. We'll know more in a little while.

"How did they get there so quickly?"

"Your friend, the Director of Alumni Affairs."

By the way, what damned fool stunt put you on top of a mountain last night?"

"Last night?"

"Yeah, you've been out for a whole day."

She tried to get out of bed.

"I want to see Dad."

"Whoa, girl, you don't have … any … clothes … on … uh…"

He managed to throw a sheet on her just in time.

"Beau, I do believe you're blushing! Haven't you ever seen a…?"

"Yes, I have, dammit. Now, put your clothes on and let me know when you're dressed."

He ran out of the room to the sound of her laughter.

"Dad, I know you can't hear me but, well, we found her. We found Lauren."

I can hear you just fine, girl.

"I'm going to tell Sheriff Fletcher. We think we know who did this but I can't tell you yet.

"Beau, his eyes fluttered! Is he able to understand me?"

She bent over the still body and kissed her father then turned away crying.

"Hey, kids, thought I'd find you here."

"Are you following us, Jake?"

"Would I do that, Beau?"

"Yeah."

"Well, just for that I won't tell you what a little birdie told me."

They stared at the old reporter and waited.

"Okay, okay, here it is. One of my sources tells me there was something unusual stuck in one of the victim's vertebrae."

"Come on, Jake, don't stretch it out."

"There was a broken off saber tip lodged in the girl's first lumbar vertebra (back bone)."

"Yes, Special Agent McCreedy, the Armory keeps records of any damaged weapons. Since we keep firearms and military weapons for training purposes, it's the law. Let's go over to the Armorer's office."

"Thank you for your cooperation, sir."

"Yes, sir. Here it is. For that year, let's see: one saber was turned in just before graduation that looked damaged and repaired. Here's the cadet's signature sheet." The Commandant blanched as he read the name.

"Are you gentlemen here for the class reunion?"

"Uh … no, son."

The flashed badges startled the gatekeeper at Moody Hall.

"Has this person signed in yet?"

"Oh, yes, sir. See that gentleman by the appetizer table? That's who you're looking for."

"Son, we don't want to intrude. Could you ask him to step out here?"

"Yes, sir."

They heard the annoyed voice and the young man's measured answer: "Sir, they're government types. Must be something important?"

"Oh, well, that's different."

They watched him move toward the doorway and step into the foyer. His uniform would have done justice to an emperor.

The two men saw the other one's name tag and nodded.

"General Passelman?"

"Yes, I'm Montgomery Passelman. What can I do for you?"

"Sheriff, Sheriff Fletcher!"

She pounded on the door while Beau shifted from one foot to the next.

"Dammit, quit makin' so much noise, girl. Come in."

The door swung open, and the old man sat staring up at the two for the second time in two days.

"Kristin, why all the fuss?"

"Sheriff Fletcher, we…"

"We found Lauren."

The gravelly voice of the man in the wheelchair became a hoarse whisper.

"Where … where was she?"

Kristin and Beau steered the wheelchair to the little front room and sat down on one of the side benches. Kristin saw the haggard look on their host's face.

"She was buried in a place she loved—up on Bluff Mountain."

"What happened to her?" He was crying now.

They both took turns filling in the details. When they had finished, Kristin put her hand on the old man's shoulder.

"We found her killer. He's probably the one who killed Ashburn, too."

Fletcher's body trembled.

"I want to see him. I want to see the man who killed my Lauren."

"Yes, sir. He's being arraigned at the courthouse today. We'll take you."

"Let me change outta these old clothes. I owe it to my daughter and wife to look decent."

"Do you need any help, sir?" Beau heard the agitation in the older man's voice.

"Don't even think about it, Jensen. I ain't a cripple, least not my hands."

They sat and waited. They heard the electric shaver hum and the rush of water in the bathroom. Ten minutes later, a different man wheeled himself into the room.

"You look great, Sheriff!"

"Yep, I can still fit in my uniform, can't I?"

"You look just like when you gave a talk at my school."

He smiled. "Beau, you remember that, huh?"

"Yes, sir!"

He didn't ask to be helped into Kristin's rental SUV. Arms trained over years easily hoisted him into the back seat. Then Beau folded his wheelchair and put it in the hatchback trunk.

shoes

The street in front of the courthouse was a zoo of activity as they pulled up. TV crews and reporters milled around the front steps. They turned as Beau got out of the car, removed the wheelchair and set it up by the back passenger side door.

"Look, it's Sheriff Fletcher!"

He barely had time to hoist himself out and into his chair before he was surrounded by the feeding-frenzied fourth estate.

"Sheriff Fletcher, Sheriff Fletcher, do you know General Passelman? Do you think he killed your daughter?"

This he was used to. How many times had he done this when he brought a perp to justice? He raised both arms, palms outward, the universal gesture that said "slow down, folks, slow down."

"Thank you for your concern. No, I have never met the general. I would certainly like to do so. But, it is up to our justice system to determine his guilt or innocence."

Come on, Fletcher, you never believed that. But the public eats that crap up.

A well-dressed civilian followed by a tall, uniformed man came to the doorway of the courthouse and walked down several steps. The reporters turned and more questions got hurled in their direction.

Fletcher knew this gambit as well: the highly-paid attorney representing the well-known perp, protesting the innocence of his client from the courthouse steps.

He studied the military man, his lawman's senses well-honed to the other's body language, the unspoken words of innocence or guilt.

chestnuts

Passelman spotted the disabled lawman stationed in his wheelchair on the sidewalk.

Piece of cake, Monty, just keep smiling.

"Please, please, let me talk with Lauren's father. I never had the chance to offer my condolences when his daughter went missing."

He walked confidently down the stairs.

I was always good at drill.

He reached the wheelchair-bound lawman and extended his hand. His face, well-schooled in dealing with military brass, assumed look number three: concern and empathy.

Fletcher took the man's outstretched right hand in his … and knew.

"Sheriff, let me…"

He felt the big hand tighten its grip on his. He felt himself being pulled closer to the man whose daughter he had butchered twenty-five years ago.

He heard the shouts.

What are they saying? I can't seem to hear them.

A .45 caliber revolver makes a thunderous noise.

He hadn't heard the cocking of the trigger in the din of the crowd.

He couldn't hear the clicks as the gun's cylinder rotated with three successive strikes of the firing pin.

General Montgomery Passelman III felt his legs dissolve as the first bullet severed his spinal cord. He felt nothing as the second bullet pierced his aorta. He was no longer alive as the third bullet

shoes

blew his now-bloodless heart out through his back.

Witnesses in the crowd later described the sheriff sitting there holding Old Betsy in his left hand. They thought he said one word before slumping forward, sliding to the ground dead.

"Lauren."

Dies Illae

"How'd you find it, Beau?"

"Newspaper morgue had the records of her burial."

They had attended the double funeral of Sheriff and Lauren Fletcher and were on one final mission.

The marker along the rural route, courtesy of the late J.B. Huffman, declared the resting place of Ottie Cline Powell. Huffman had memorialized the child in his booklet *Little Boy Lost in the Mountains of Virginia* back in 1925.

But the whereabouts of Ottie's mother remained a mystery.

Kristin was a driven woman. She had to find the grave site.

Beau gave in.

He drove her to an isolated area and began to count off his footsteps until he suddenly stopped.

"It's supposed to be here, Kristin."

She removed the gold locket from her blouse pocket and knelt down on the dry earth. Beau handed her a small garden trowel, which she used to dig a shallow hole in the dirt.

She placed the locket in it and covered it up.

Jensen could barely hear her whispered words.

"Your son needs you."

Beau helped Kristin to her feet. He stared in wonder at the young woman he had met only days before.

Call it hunch; call it intuition, he knew: this was the woman he would marry one day.

His cell phone buzzed.

"We'd better get back to the hospital. Your dad's taken a turn for the worse."

shoes

Transcendence

She sat in what the hospital staff called the Go to Jesus room. Large hospitals always maintain a few to warehouse the terminal patients, the ones with no time left to be transferred to a hospice center.

"Beau, he's smiling."

"It's almost as if he's reached some closure and knows it."

She started to cry.

What could he say? Once more he resorted to the only helpful response he knew: he held her.

They make a handsome couple, don't they, Gus?

My Kristin was always a beauty. Her guy looks pretty decent, too. And that reminds me, mysterious spirit guide, what now? Are you my Virgil, come to lead me to the underworld of Hades?

Wrong sex, big boy.

My Beatrice? Never thought I'd wind up in Paradise.

Ever so slowly the raven-haired girl appeared before him.

Do I look like a Virgil to you, Brother Rat?

Oh, God! Lauren!

You can be so dense even when you're dying, Gus.

So, you're the one playing my Ghost of Gustmas past, huh? But, who's the kid next to you?

Don't you know me, sir?

You're little Ottie!

Yes, sir.

Ottie, what really happened to you? Can you tell me?

Spirits have ears and Gus leaned over as the little boy whispered in his.

Never would have guessed that, kid!

Hey, doofus, remember me?

Ashburn, Donnie Ashburn!

It's almost over for me, Gus. To steal a quote from that bastard, Passelman, there's just one little loose end. Come on, guys, I'll show you.

"Miss Mayhugh?"

"You the guy they call the Commandant?"

"Yes, ma'am."

The distinguished soldier stood in the entryway to the little antique shop in Lexington.

What do I say? What can I say? Even 'Nam wasn't this bad.

"Well?"

He cleared his throat.

"What happened to Cadet Ashburn was a singular and tragic event in the history of our school. We, the entire board, wish to reinstate your … uh … nephew on the rolls as an honored cadet."

"Huh, won't do him no good. He's been dead twenty five years."

Yes it will, Ma! Listen to him. He's going to clear my name!

She stood there, listening to what only a mother's heart can hear.

"Miss Mayhugh, are you feeling well?"

"Uh … yes, Mr. Commandant. On behalf of Donnie, I accept."

Way to go, Ma!

Well, Gus, Lauren, I gotta go. See you shortly.

Bye, Donnie.

Okay, Brother Rat, you ready now?

Why is he a rat, Miss Lauren?

Because he's a VMI graduate, Ottie.

I don't get it.

Well, I'm a Brother Rat, too.

But, but, you're a girl!

Perceptive little tyke, isn't he? Listen, kid, it's a title, a badge of fellowship and honor for surviving the rigors of our school. At VMI, any member of your class who makes it through the tortures of the Rat Line and then Breakout is your Brother Rat for life.

And afterwards, too, Ottie.

What about me?

What about what, squirt?

Are you going to leave me?

Aren't you coming with us, Ottie?

I can't, Miss Lauren. I haven't been able to find my mama.

Hmmm. Lauren, how does this sound to you? What say we make Ottie, here, an….

Even spirits can whisper.

Two shadows nodded.

Okay, kid, listen up. By the power invested in me and Lauren by … what power do we have, Lauren?

He did make it through his own forest Rat Line, and Bluff Mountain was his Breakout, Gus.

That should do it.

Okay, then by the power invested in us as Brother Rats, and being dead as well, we—Lauren Fletcher and Augustus Belmont— hereby make you, Ottie Kline Powell , an Honorary Brother Rat!

Uh, maybe that should be Ratling?

Shut up, Gus!

Oh, wow!

The kid looks good in ducks and dyke, doesn't he, Lauren?

Ottie, Ottie, liebchen!

Mama? Mama, Mama, look, look at me! I'm a Brother Rat!

Look at him run!

That kid would have beaten the pants off us in obstacle course, Gus.

He made it up a mountain.

Our mountain awaits, Brother Rat.

Race ya to the top.

You're on, slowpoke.

Hey, wait, Lauren, the kid left us something.

What, Gus?

Chestnuts.

The heart monitor played a solitary bugle note.

Postscript

"Hey, drummer boy, I didn't know you could play that well."

"You weren't too bad, either bugle boy."

"Ever think we'd see a day like this?"

"Gotta admit, never heard of a "roll-in.""

"Yeah, a ceremony for two dead cadets. Strange.

"Hey, you carvin' another notch on your sticks? Thought you only did that with rollouts."

"Nope, no notches. This time it's a smiley face."

shoes

Prologue

The fields and jungle floors lie fallow now, fertile from countless years of decaying organic matter… and the blood of young men dying in old men's wars.

1864

He died that mid-May day.

He was barely seventeen years old and a day's horseback ride from home.

He died shoeless.

1964

He died that mid-May day.

He was twenty-three and half and a world away from home.

Rain

He died shoeless.

1864

The clouds cried for three days.

The roads were wagon-wheel ruts of mud, horse droppings and debris.

His company, his friends, ignored the sucking sounds, until the quick-sand mud sucked their boots and wool socks off.

1964

The C-131 transport landed at Cam Ranh Bay field that late September, 1963 day.

The humidity was drenching as he and his company disembarked.

It added to the flop-sweat rings on his fatigues.

He felt his feet sliding on the insides of his boots.

The old timers at the base laughed at the newbies.

"Wait'll you see what the monsoons do, kid."

As It Was in the Beginning

The soil-stained skull grinned at him.

It sat perched on the pair of mildewed field combat boots in the small, antique French portmanteau on his desk.

Was it only ten minutes ago that life as he knew it had ended?

Two senior cadets sat nervously in the small receptionist's office. An odor of decay emanated from the antique box lying next to the young Asian female cadet. Her partner, a lean, olive-skinned boy, politely enquired once more of the Commandant's secretary.

"Please, ma'am; please let him know we're here."

He really is busy, but I'll try, cadet."

She stood, walked the three steps from her small, gun-metal gray desk and knocked gently on the frosted glass-windowed door. Gilt letters spelled out COMMANDANT NATHANIEL BERKSON.

She heard the "come in" and entered.

"Commandant…"

"Yes, Miller?"

He wondered why she didn't use the intercom. She had been his right hand for years, so he trusted her judgment. The look on her face confirmed it.

"Two seniors (first-year cadets) to see you, sir. They both insist it is of the utmost urgency."

He shook his head then reconsidered, as Miller added, "they brought a box with them, sir. The thing scares me."

Miller wasn't easily scared. She had single-handedly saved his life in Saigon by taking out two Viet Cong assassins stalking him.

He stared at her gray eyes and graying hair.

"Okay, show them in."

Two cadets in their final year entered the small, well-kept office, braced and saluted smartly.

He recognized them as Cadet Kiran Bhatia and Cadet Thu Vu Pham. Top of their class and, from the looks of it, probably going to have a crossed-swords wedding ceremony at the chapel on graduation day.

"Sir … uh … I … uh … we regret disturbing you, but Cadet Pham received a package that…."

The young man looked at the young woman, and Berkson saw the love between them. Bhatia was obviously descended from the warrior caste of India. Six feet tall with black, penetrating eyes matching an olive complexion that only Mother India could produce. The Commandant had met his father, a Supreme Court justice, and his grandfather, a legendary figure in the international world, at Bhatia's entrance to VMI.

Pham, ah yes, he recognized that look too. She was the truly aristocratic descendant of Vietnam. Somewhere in her family line a Frenchman had shared his DNA. But the cadet, normally placid even in the most adverse conditions, was overtly agitated.

"Sir," she blurted out, "I received a special package three days ago. It was sent on behalf of my grandfather's attorneys. I…."

Her eyes welled up.

Bhatia took over. "It's a small trunk, sir. Thu's grandfather passed away several months ago while revisiting his village."

He then mentioned a name that caused Berkson to blanch, but he remained silent.

Pham composed herself. "It's a long story, sir. Back in the war, my paternal great-great-grandfather was the chief, the leader of our small rural village. He acted as liaison between our group and the ARVIN (Army of the Republic of Vietnam) and their U.S. Special Forces advisers…."

Once more she hesitated. Her keen eyes swept the décor in the office and spotted the Green Beret resting in a place of honor on a shelf behind the Commandant's desk. Numerous medals, field combat ribbons and more joined in chorus.

"We brought the box here, sir," Bhatia interjected. "May we bring it in?"

The old soldier had turned gray. His lean, six-foot-two-inch frame seemed to hunch over. He knew. His mind screamed "Oh, God, no!" but he waved them to bring in the box.

Bhatia quickly exited to Miller's office and returned carrying a two-by two feet miniature French portmanteau. He hefted it onto Berkson's desk and stepped back.

Pham reached into her tunic and removed an old-fashioned iron key. Unspoken permission crossed between her leader and herself, and she inserted the key into the heavy brass fitting that served as closure and lock. With a twisted scraping, iron springs turned within and the latch popped open. A familiar odor, one the old soldier had smelled many times during his military career, permeated the room.

He knew it well: the odor of the grave.

"Sir, I know you will understand why I brought it to you when you see the contents."

shoes

Berkson's hands reached forward slowly, raising the teak and variegated metal top and gazed within.

Death was no stranger to him. He had seen his share of dead and dying comrades, from Vietnam through the early Middle East wars. The grinning skull meant nothing by itself.

What turned his hair were the combat boots and the verdigrised oval bronze belt buckle lying on the bottom of the trunk. He knew that buckle, a historic symbol of the school he served. It bore the letters VMI.

He also knew why the skull grinned back at him.

Pham's voice continued the oral history, but he didn't need to hear it. He had lived it. He sat at the desk, fixated by that remnant of the man he had known, and he relived the story in his soul.

"Ashburn, Berkson, congratulations."

They stood at attention as their commander, Colonel Enfante, placed the coveted Green Berets on their heads. They were Special Forces now.

"Whaddya say, Nate, a three-way wedding?"

He stared at his friend, Lonnie Ashburn. They had survived the Rat Line at VMI together with Lon's twin brother, Sam. Both Ashburn boys had dated the twin Mayhugh girls while Nate was sweet on another local girl.

"I dunno, Lon, I'll bet we won't have the time. Most likely we're gonna be, quote, advisers somewhere in Asia the way things are going."

It was early 1963 and President John F. Kennedy had upped

the ante in Vietnam by increasing the number of military advisers sent to instruct the ARVIN. Kennedy wanted to avoid the failure of the former French occupiers and their disastrous defeat by the Vietnamese at Dien Bien Phu in 1953.

Vietnam was the classic military tar baby. Its leaders were despised even by the normally placid Buddhist priests, the Bonze, who immolated themselves in protest. They, too, joined the insurgent North Vietnamese.

"Besides," Nate continued, "I don't think Sam's up to it. He didn't make it."

The two young VMI grads nodded.

They had leave time. They left Fort Benning, Georgia, and headed back to Lexington, Virginia. Both guys gave knowing grins as they split up, heading off to different sections of the town. Each knew where the other was going.

"Abby!"

She melted in his muscular arms. It had been so long and now he seemed to appear at her door by magic. He had written to her, almost daily. Those missives were precious to her. But now he was here!

They danced and dreamed together that night.

"Nate … uh … I didn't know you were coming."

He knew something was wrong the moment he spotted the Chevy convertible in front of her house. He hadn't called. He wanted to surprise her.

He did.

The petite brunette elementary school teacher tried her best to block his view into the house she shared with her parents. It didn't work.

He spotted the other guy standing by the settee.

"I'm sorry, Maggie, I didn't mean to disturb you. Give my best to your parents … and Tim."

He headed back to the digs he shared with Lonnie Ashburn. He knew that his friend wouldn't be back that night.

He lay on his bed, clad only in army-green shorts, and stared at the ceiling.

Glory 1864

"We're goin' in, ain't we?"

They whispered as all soldiers do when their sergeant isn't looking.

"Sergeant, assemble the men."

"Yes, sir."

"Companies A, B, C and D, fall in."

It was raining that day. The sky alternated between platinum and dark gray. Large black clouds moved about, emptying their water-filled bladders in heavy downpours.

"Guess we're a goin."

"Yep."

"Scared?"

"Nope. Uh … are you?"

"Uh-unh."

They were comforted in each other's lie.

They were shaggy-dog wet, as they approached their destination.

The town was gathered to greet their young men.

The rain had stopped, and the May heat and valley winds soon dried them off. Now they strutted their manhood down the main street, snare drums rat-a-tat-tatting, drum sticks twirling, as they were tossed in the air to impress the young ladies of the local Episcopal Women's Seminary cheering them on.

She caught his eye. They had met once before at an arranged social between the seminary and the Barracks students.

He was once more smitten.

That evening she quietly escaped the duenna eyes of the

school mistress and came to a large poplar tree near the bivouac area.

He heard the female owl call and quietly arose from his comrades snoring watch.

She hugged him.

That night they became one.

He arose and reached into his side pocket. It was the only thing he could give her, the 18-karat-gold, French fuse repeater watch his father and mother had given him. He pressed it into her hands and kissed her again. He kissed her and asked her to carry his watch always. If he didn't return, well, its ticking would remind her of his heartfelt love.

She startled him by taking his whittling knife. She reached up and cut a lock of his hair and placed it within the outer hunter's case of the pocket watch. Then she cut off a curl of her own hair, tied it and placed it in the tunic pocket above his heart.

She kissed him once more and then both departed, she to sneak back into the parsonage, he to pretend to lie quietly next to the smoldering camp fire.

The young women heard the hill-echoed artillery that fateful May day.

In the distance they saw the smoke rise in the now-cloudless sky.

He stood with his mates, clutching the loaded long rifle. He was afraid.

He spotted the breach in the gray ranks and saw his friends run forward to fill it.

He did not hesitate. As he ran full charge, the water-logged soil of the farm turned battleground sucked off his shoes and stockings.

He felt the piercing pain as the Minié ball tore through his tunic chest pocket. It entered his chest and penetrated his aorta.

He felt his heart as it sped up then stopped.

Her lock of hair now lay within his heart forever.

Her hand closed tightly on the pocket watch in her blouse. She stifled a scream as she felt the knife-like pain pierce the left side of her chest.

She knew.

She knew soon after finishing her matriculation at the Women's Seminary in June.

She could not stain the honor of her family or the memory of that soldier boy and the child that lay within her.

She accepted the hand of the eager young man who had courted her in the past.

She was now the wife of the Honorable Eustace Mayhugh, attorney at law.

The boychild who entered the world eight months later became her only solace.

Glory 1964

"Send a squad to…"

The major noted the name of the outlying village in alpha quadrant then looked up at the colonel.

"Trouble, Zach?"

"Yeah, the Intel boys say there's been increased Cong penetration up there. I dunno, Reid, is this worth it?"

Sterett hesitated. He, too, felt the futility of trying to help in a country that hated its own leadership. But theirs was not to reason why.

"Got anyone who knows the area?"

"Two. Ashburn and Berkson. Both top notch, both have worked the area and know the village people."

"Okay, you know what to do."

"I'll send Berkson. Ashburn's men just came in off patrol."

Sterett rose. He saw Catterton's shoulders slumped, his forehead creased in worry lines. He knew that feeling, too. When you not only walk but live in the valley of the shadow of death, those you work with become more than brothers.

Yeah, there were morons. Some spit-and-polish academy types didn't seem to give a shit when they sacrificed their own men in gung ho maneuvers, but Special Forces guys weren't like that.

Too bad the spit-and-polish types didn't learn when their own men took them out.

He sighed and shook his head then called his sergeant.

"Get Berkson over here."

"Sorry, sir, Captain Berkson was just taken to Saigon. I think he's going to be operated on."

"What the hell happened?"

"Dunno, sir, he was talking with some of his guys then he doubled over like he was pole-axed. One of the medics thinks his appendix burst."

"Shit! Okay, get me Ashburn."

"Captain Berkson, we're gonna need to take your appendix out."

He lay there in the field hospital. The young surgeon peering down at him through gown and face mask didn't sound like he had started puberty yet, but he seemed to know what he was doing.

"Okay, now breathe deeply."

The anesthesia induction mask was placed over his face by a medic and he started to breathe. Despite the morphine they had given him, it was agonizing at first, that burning, penetrating right lower quadrant belly pain. Then, nothing.

He awoke, now lying in a field hospital bed. He felt nauseated, dizzy.

"Feeling better?"

She hovered in his field of view.

Must be the pain meds. Didn't realize Army nurses looked this good.

She laughed, as she saw the sheet over his legs start to rise.

"Why, Captain Berkson, I guess the guys were right. You are a dirty old man after all."

"What? Oh, shit!" he croaked.

He managed to look down and saw the source of her merriment. He turned red.

Her name tag read MILLER.

His mouth was dry, his neck still aching from the endotracheal tube that had been shoved down his throat after he had undergone anesthesia.

"How … long?"

"It'll be awhile but you'll be back with your men in a few weeks."

"But…."

"Don't worry about it. I hear there's an even bigger stud out there at your camp who's filling in."

"Lonnie?"

"Yeah, that's what I heard. Captain Ashburn."

"Ashburn, you know about this village?"

"Yes, sir. We've been out that way several times. The chief is a nice old guy. Hates the VC for killing his son.

"Good. Now, remember, the VC are moving more men in there, so watch your six."

"Yes, sir. Uh, how's Nate?"

"He's doing fine, Ashburn. From what I hear, he's keeping the nurses in stitches."

Both men laughed.

Sterett watched, as Ashburn called his squad together. They checked out each other's gear then headed out. The major belched and went back to reading recon reports.

They moved carefully. The jungle underbrush could conceal very lethal pitfalls. Deep holes lined with sharpened stakes coated with human feces that would impale the unwary who walked over carefully placed vegetation mats meant to conceal them. Bouncing Betty mines that, when tripped flew up to waist level before detonating. And more devilish maiming and deadly gadgets.

They faced an enemy who could survive on a bowl of rice a day and live off the land or under it. Compounding that was that the VC could easily fade into the surrounding village people until ready to strike again. Even the women VC were deadly.

They came to the village edge and stopped. All communication was by hand signals until an all-clear status was established.

"Captain Lonnie, Captain Lonnie!"

The young boy, fourteen maybe, came running toward them.

He knew it was safe then.

"Khai, you've grown just since last time!"

He patted the boy's head and slipped him a candy bar. The chief's grandson had a real sweet tooth.

The boy led him to his grandfather's hut. Ashburn greeted the old man, as he came out to welcome him.

Later, over a bowl of pho served by Khai, the two men spoke of enemy movements, the welfare of the village and how much the boy had grown.

Nguyen Khai (family name before given name) ran his small hand over the buckle on Ashburn's belt.

"What is VMI, Captain Lonnie?"

"It's where I went to school, Khai. It is a school that trains great warriors and leaders of my people."

"Why don't the others have that?"

The tall American laughed. "Well, Khai, first off, they didn't go there. And second, it's not official Army issue. It's my good luck charm. It was given to me by Captain Nate. You remember Captain Nate, don't you?"

"Yes, sir. Did he go to this VMI?"

"You bet, kid. Someday we'll tell you about being Brother Rats."

Khai was startled.

"You do not look like river rat, Captain Lonnie!"

No one noticed the quiet villager silently leave the village boundaries.

And no one saw him return.

"Thank you again, Nguyen Phong.

Khai, thank you for cleaning my boots."

He carefully pulled the combat boots on and laced them up."

Ashburn shook the chief's hand, signaled his men and began to move out.

"Nate, when are you going to call me Martha or Marty or ... oh, I don't know!"

He looked down at the girl he kept calling Miller. She had an amazing way of pouting, her gray eyes and silver-blond hair flashing in the Saigon sun. He was walking around now, nearly healed from his appendectomy, and they had stopped off at a sidewalk vendor of noodles and pho, the Vietnamese equivalent of Ramen and fish soup.

He grinned and continued to slurp the pho down with gusto.

Suddenly, her voice dropped.

"Don't move, Nate!"

His shoulders tightened as he felt her grab his service .45.

Two loud reports shook his ears.

He turned and saw the two black, pajama-clad VC lying in the road, their foreheads blown off and their automatic pistols unfired.

He dropped his soup bowl and hugged the now-trembling young nurse.

Ashburn and his squad moved back along the jungle trail to the pickup site. The Hueys (helicopters) would be there. The squad remained vigilant, but their stalkers knew the area far better.

A hand signal from the starvation-thin VC lieutenant and his five men raised high-powered rifles. A volley of shots rang out.

Ashburn saw five of his men knocked forward, their heads almost non-existent. By reflex he moved one step before starting to drop when he felt the trip wire of the hidden mine move under his foot.

His last conscious thought was "Oh, shit!" before the explosion hurled him backwards, the impact yanking him out of his boots.

He didn't hear the V.C. lieutenant stand at his head.

He didn't feel the whooshing impact of the machete as it came down and severed his head from the rest of his mangled body.

His head felt no pain as it was impaled on a post stuck in the ground.

Nguyen Khai was shaking. He had witnessed the slaughter and recognized the Cong Lieutenant as the same man who had tortured and killed his father. He remained quiet, hidden from view, trying to plot out both his escape and a death strategy against that VC soldier.

He didn't have to worry.

Two of Ashburn's squad had survived the withering fire. Wounded, playing dead, they suddenly rose and took out the VC squad in a volley of shots. The lieutenant they saved for last.

He lay wounded in all four extremities, as two grim-faced Green Berets approached him.

It wasn't too hard to take his machete away.

It was even easier to remove his head the same way he had done to Ashburn.

The only difference was that he was alive when the whoosh of the blade came down on his neck.

They didn't see the young boy who had grabbed the Captain's boots, belt buckle and head. They were too filled with the blood lust of revenge.

The boy sat behind his grandfather's hut and stroked the head of the man he had called Captain Lonnie. He whispered in the dead man's ear.

"I will bury you here. I will honor you always."

The recovery team brought back ten bodies, one of them headless.

Berkson wept that day.

Dearly Beloved

"Come on, Kristin, we're gonna be late!"

"Quit fussing, Beau. We've got plenty of time."

"You know how my mother is, Kris. I swear she has a stopwatch in her brain. Besides, we don't want to keep General and Mrs. Green waiting."

Kristin Belmont looked at her future husband and smiled.

It's only two weeks away.

Beau Jensen looked at his future bride and smiled back.

Has it only been eight months?

"You sure you want to be Mrs. Beau Jensen?"

"It's got a nice ring to it."

The fingers of her right hand caressed the engagement ring he had given her.

"And, speaking of ringing, there goes that damned phone!" he exclaimed.

She flipped open her cell phone.

"Kristin Belmont soon-to-be Jensen speaking. Who's calling?"

She had laughed as she said it, but her expression changed instantly.

Beau watched his fiancée carefully. She had that look again.

"Yes, Ms. Miller, I understand. We'll stop by on our way to the chapel. It's our rehearsal day."

She blushed, as she heard the older woman offer both apologies for disturbing her and profuse congratulations.

"You and the Commandant are coming, aren't you?"

Beau heard the "wouldn't miss it for the world" come through Kristin's phone loud and clear.

"Okay, wife-to-be, what's up now? Is the Canterville Ghost haunting the Barracks?"

"Uh … Beau, I don't think he was headless, was he?"

Beau Jensen had become, as of May 6th, a graduate of the University of Virginia. August would bring orientation and the start of his new life as a medical student at UVA. In another two weeks, he would be married.

It was May 8th, wedding practice day at the chapel.

Does life really move this quickly?

Was it only eight months ago that he had met the spunky young woman and her dying father on Bluff Mountain? Was it just a twinkling in time since they—no, she—had solved two, twenty-five-year-old murders and restored honor to a dead Virginia Military Institute cadet and his family?

How could I not fall in love with her?

When he had told Jake Williams, the old reporter at the *Lexington News Gazette*, that he had proposed, Jake turned with a knowing grin, slapped the tall college grad and emergency medical tech on the back, and laughed as he said "what took ya so long, kid?"

His father's response was typical, as he stood in the living room of the real estate magnate's large home.

"Well, now you'll have to get a real job and drop this medical school nonsense. There's always a place for you at my office."

An "I told you so" lay unspoken on the older man's face.

His mother had muttered a "hush up, Gunther," to her husband

and took Beau's hands in hers. Her head tilted upward to look into her son's eyes.

"She's a lovely girl, Beau. But isn't it a bit … uh … sudden? Your father and I were engaged for three years before we married. Is there something you're not telling us?"

He blushed then fought to control the rage that made his blush pale in comparison.

"No, Mom, she's not pregnant."

Hermione Jensen uttered a "Thank God. What would my friends have said?"

Beau turned to leave then looked over his shoulder and called out, "Oh, Dad, don't worry. The tuition's taken care of. You won't need to spend a penny."

Gunther Jensen raised an eyebrow.

"Did you win the lottery, son?"

"Dr. Shepland took care of it."

Beau was halfway out the door, when he heard his mother's plaintive whine.

"Gunther, dear, I can't seem to find my taupe shoes. Have you seen them?"

Beau's next stop was the office of Dr. Richard Shepland, his mentor, confidant, and guardian angel when it came to Beau's career decision.

Shepland was old now, well past the age when the average guy would hang it up. But, as he never stopped telling Beau, "I'll work as long as I'm still learning and still having fun."

shoes   145

The old doctor listened and smiled, as Beau kept repeating himself about his wedding plans, and how he couldn't thank him enough for picking up the tuition tab.

"Slow down, boy, slow down. That's what money's for. And, yes I'll be there at your wedding rehearsal; and wedding. But where is 'there?'"

"Oh, geez, Doc, I forgot, didn't I? It's at the VMI chapel."

"How did you manage to swing that? You're not an alumnus."

"It was kinda special. I mean, you know Kristin, right? Well, she spoke with Ms. Green in the Alumni Office and, all of a sudden, that's where it would be held."

"How does your fiancée like working at VMI?"

That was another blessing from heaven, compliments of the Alumni Office.

"Have you met anyone from Kristin's family, besides her late father?"

"I went to her graduation at William and Mary. It was just me and her uncle Denny—General Denzil Johnson. He was a roommate and Brother Rat to her dad."

"Didn't her mother show up?"

"No, seems she's on a cruise with her new boyfriend."

"Is she going to come to the wedding?"

"We sent her an invitation and Kristin called her but…."

Beau suspected that her mother never forgave her for going with her father on his last journey.

Shepland nodded. He had seen it too many times during his career.

"Doc, you will be there, won't you? I mean the rehearsal and the wedding."

"Yes, Beau, and I'll be at your White Coat Ceremony at the medical school in August, too."

"Thanks, Doc."

He hugged the old man and ran out the door.

That and more crossed the young man's mind as he stared at his future mate.

"Headless? What the hell's going on? Do they have another ghost to exorcise?"

"It's probably nothing. The Commandant's secretary said the cadets are seeing a headless mangled body wandering through the Barracks hallways after Taps and lights out."

"So?"

"She wondered if we could help. She says the Commandant is … uh … very disturbed by the 'manifestation.' I think we should swing by there before chapel and get some of the lowdown."

It was the most important day before the wedding: rehearsal day—a dress rehearsal in jeans at the chapel.

"Kris, come on!"

"I'm ready!," she said, as she suddenly noticed his feet.

"Wait, Beau, you aren't going to wear those, are you?"

He looked at his sneakers.

"Why not? It's just a practice."

"Please, honey, wear your black shoes."

We Are Gathered

"Dang! Now where did you put your shoes, old woman?"

I must be getting old. I'm talking to myself now.

Abigail Mayhugh turned the OPEN sign to CLOSED and locked the front door of her little antique shop in Lexington then headed back to her bedroom in the back of the store.

She washed and changed out of her dull-gray house dress. It was almost a uniform that she had worn daily for years.

No, Abigail, you need to dress up for those two young 'uns.

She took the ceil blue dress from her closet. She had last worn it when her Donnie's name was cleared in the special VMI ceremony last year.

She owed it to Kris and Beau to show up for the wedding rehearsal and the wedding. She smiled, as she remembered how the young couple had come by personally to invite her. Her heart fluttered as she heard the words young Kristin had called her: "Aunt Abby." That very day she had called her lawyer and changed her will. The kids would be her legal heirs.

The tinkling of the sleigh bells hung on the storefront door interrupted her thoughts.

Thought I locked that door.

She yelled out, "We're closed."

The bells jingled again.

"Dang, double dang!"

She padded out front in her slippers.

"Who's there?"

No answer.

She went to the front door. It was still locked. She opened it and looked up and down the street.

No delivery trucks, no cars.

Nothing.

She locked it again.

As she turned around, she spotted a small box on the counter. It wasn't there before.

Not expecting any deliveries.

She went over and picked it up.

Cardboard, marbleized color, old. The lid came off easily. Inside a gold pocket watch reflected the dim store light.

"Huh, you did forget again, old woman. Don't you remember sending out Papa's pocket watch to be cleaned and serviced?"

The mid-19th century pocket watch gleamed in her hands. Pre-Civil War period, solid gold, it had been passed on from father to son, starting with Great Grandpa Eustace. Her father had only twin girls, so Abigail got the watch, and her sister got some of their mother's jewelry.

She nodded. "Perfect gift for Beau."

She stuffed the box in her dress pocket, went back to her bedroom, and sat down on her bed.

Now, where did I put my shoes?

Slowly she got down on arthritic knees and looked under her bed.

Ah, got you, you little devils!

She slung the errant shoes on the bed but didn't get up.

The storage box called out to her. *Open me.*

She slid it out and reentered the door to her past.

Her boy, Donnie, smiled back at her from the gilt-framed photo, proudly wearing his cadet uniform.

"You're finally at rest, now, boy."

She kissed the glass-enclosed picture then picked up another frame.

My mausoleum of love.

A somewhat older young man, almost the twin of her Donnie, in Army uniform and Green Beret, seemed to blow a kiss at her. The carefully printed words at the bottom tore at her.

"Love you forever, Abby."

She held the framed photo next to her heart.

"Lonnie, Lonnie, did you know you had a son?"

She rocked back and forth, his picture tightly pressed against her chest, reliving that last night before he left.

"You know I have to leave, Abby."

"Couldn't we … uh … get married? We could go to the Justice of the Peace. Maybe my sister and Sam could come, too."

Once more she saw his head shaking. He held her.

The old woman cried silently and alone.

"Okay, Abigail Mayhugh, pull yourself together. You can't disappoint those kids."

She placed the framed pictures back in the box and slid it back under the bed. She straightened her dress, brushed back a few strands of gray hair.

She opened the door, stepped out, inhaled deeply, and relocked it.

"Maybe Kristin and Beau will have the life I never had."

In the Presence of God

The gray-eyed woman was intimidating.

I can't begin to imagine what this woman's life was like.

Kristin thought about the Commandant's secretary, as she sat once more in the anteroom to his office.

That first time, nine months before, had been bad enough. But now there was something, some miasma that filled the room.

"Ms. Belmont, I'm not sure where to begin, but the way you helped us with the Ashburn boy, well, Ms. Green said I should call you."

Kristin felt that familiar knot in her gut.

Beau stood by her side, protective and concerned.

"Ms. Miller, can we cut to the chase?" he said. "We've got a wedding rehearsal in one hour."

Miller smiled knowingly. She had experienced the same protectiveness years before. It had never really ended between her and Berkson.

"Yes, cut to the chase I will, young man. Strange as it seems it may well involve an Ashburn."

"But Donnie was cleared," Kristin blurted out.

"Not Donnie, Kristin. Lonnie Ashburn, his father."

Kristin closed her eyes. She knew the old woman's secret. She had revealed Abigail Mayhugh's connection the last time she was here.

Miller continued.

"The Commandant and Lon Ashburn were Brother Rats and the best of friends. They served in Vietnam together. Nate got sick—appendicitis—the day he was supposed to take a patrol out.

Lonnie took his place.

He never returned, until today."

"You mean, he's alive? My God, we should tell Aunt Abby."

"Uh … not quite, Kris. That's why I asked you here."

Martha Miller stood up.

"I called you because there have been reports of a headless specter walking the halls of the Barracks the past several days. I think I know why."

She knocked on the Commandant's door, heard the familiar "come in," and beckoned the couple to follow her.

Kristin took one step into the room. The miasma was now a black wall. It engulfed her, and Beau had to catch her before she fell. He carried her to a chair and placed her carefully in it.

Her mind cleared.

She saw the miniature portmanteau sitting on Berkson's desk. Berkson stood and stared at it.

Miller stepped forward and turned the box around to face the girl.

Slowly, she opened the lid.

Kristin saw the cone of light emanating upwards. It took the form of a military man. She had seen that face before.

Three people sat spellbound, as Kristin rose, approached the box and held out her hands. They saw nothing.

Kristin Belmont stared at the handsome face. A thought crossed her mind.

Yes, you truly are Donnie's father.

Where's my Abby?

It was a thunderbolt that rocked her. She steadied herself.

She will be here today in the chapel.

Ah!

Young woman, tell my friend he was not to blame.

The light dwindled down. Now only the skull stared at her.

To Witness

The great mural bore testimony to that fateful May day in 1864.

The flags of various states lined the lateral walls.

The Spartan oak pews bordered the nave to the chancel.

"Is everyone here?"

Wedding planners have to be fussy, obsessive compulsive nit pickers. They are the recipients of countless bridal tears and mother of the bride hand wringing if everything is not perfect.

"Beau, you're still wearing sneakers!"

He grinned sheepishly. "Yeah, it's better than poking a thumb in certain people's eyes."

She tried to turn furtively. Yes, his parents were sitting in the back. Now, she stared at the chapel *in toto* and was amazed to see how many of the staff she had gotten to know since working at the institute. And this was only the dress rehearsal.

She smiled, as the women raised hands in thumbs-up salute.

She crossed her fingers. Was that one special person present?

The old lady sat quietly in the back row, her ceil blue dress fitting loosely over a food-deprived body. No one had deprived her. She had, as she was fond of saying, the appetite of a sparrow.

Kristin walked back and hugged the old woman.

"Thank you, Abby. I know it's not easy for you to travel."

Abigail Mayhugh looked at Kristin. *Would I have had a daughter like this?*

"Girl, give this to your young man. It's been in my family for generations."

She handed over the aged, marbleized cardboard box.

Kristin opened it, gasped and hugged her again.

"Come on, people," the wedding planner called out in exasperation. "I know this is just a rehearsal, but practice makes perfect, right?"

Kristin sighed and lined up at the back of a small retinue of bridesmaids.

The wedding planner began to hum the processional music and the party moved forward. As they approached the altar, Kristin stopped and stared.

The mural was swirling in mist. The field of lost shoes was now a jungle.

Two others saw it.

The young army officer, Green Beret cocked to the side, smiled and extended his arms and beckoned.

Abigail stood, her own arms outstretched.

"Lonnie, Lonnie!"

The third observer stood ramrod straight. His right arm came up in full salute. His whisper was heard only by Kristin.

"Forgive me, Lon."

The figure turned and smiled, and gave an off the forehead salute. Once more he extended his arms, and a second figure appeared in the mural. A young woman in ceil blue smiled radiantly at her lover. He, in turn, placed his arms around her.

The party turned as the sound of a falling object.

"Abby!"

Kristin ran to the back pew and held her in her arms. Beau and Dr. Shepland looked at each other and shook their heads.

"Kris," Beau whispered, "she's gone."

Postscript: Let No Man Put Asunder

The modern day Pieta cast little shadow in the midday sun that May 15th.

Mr. and Mrs. Beau and Kristin Belmont Jensen gazed at Sir Moses Ezekiel's statue of Virginia Mourning Her Dead.

Beside them stood Martha Miller.

The Cadet Commander read the names of those who had fallen or died as a result of wounds at the Battle of New Market on May 15, 1864.

With each name a cadet stepped forward, saluted, and answered:

"Died on the field of honor, sir!"

The last name and response in the doxology rang out.

Kristin took Martha Miller's hand.

The cadet paused then called out in strident cadence: "Lon Ashburn."

Nathaniel Berkson stepped forward, saluted and replied:

"Died on the field of honor, sir!"

Special thanks to the man who wishes to be known only as "Leonidas," and to Mrs. Carole Green, VMI Director of Alumni Affairs who is not, and is no relation to, the alumni director in the story, except in an amazing coincidence—honest!—and who is even more gracious than her fictitious counterpart.

shoes